# NEMESIS

(The Nemesis Series Book I)

L.J. MARTIN

WOLFPACK
PUBLISHING
— EST 2013 —

**Nemesis**
**(The Nemesis Series Book I)**

L. J. Martin

Wolfpack Publishing
6032 Wheat Penny Avenue
Las Vegas, NV 89122

ISBN: 978-1-88533-928-7

*For Mike Bray*
*Old friends lost and found again often age like*
*good wine...*

# NEMESIS

## Chapter One

IT'S BEEN fifteen years since I've killed a man.

At least a man against whom I held a grudge, the recent unpleasantries excluded, as in the smoke and haze of battle you seldom saw the face of a man you dispatched. And that whole affair seemed President Lincoln's grudge and only my duty as a sworn soldier...not that the taste in your mouth is any sweeter for the small difference. After all, killing is killing. But that man fifteen years ago, when I was a young man of only fifteen years, came against my family, and he was well known to me and mine.

I have now carefully cleaned and sighted my weapons again, and cast a few bullets, as I have a task before me.

But I hoped the task would never shadow my door nor sour the taste in my mouth again. I'd hoped no man would offend or threaten me or mine so much I'd feel the need...the requirement...to put them in hell.

The devil of it is it looks like I now have an even half-dozen lowlifes on my list of chores.

Five of the six offenders, seeming dry and dusty, rode into my sister's homestead, three hundred twenty acres in the middle of thousands more of federal free-graze land, feigning needing the well for their horses and their own parched throats. Sarah McBain MacIntosh was as fine an upstanding Christian woman, a lady, a sister—and at one time a friend—as God ever created, and would never turn a man away from a mere drink of water or a hot meal for that matter.

Old Ignacio Sanchez, whom I'd met only once, related her story to me via a very hard-to-read letter.

The worthless scum repaid my sister's hospitality by back shooting her husband like a cur dog, in turn cutting down my sister as she went for the scattergun to defend children and home, then burning their place to the ground with my two beautiful angel nieces still inside—angels whose presence I was never blessed with, except at a long distance, and whom I never had a chance to give so much as an uncle's hug.

And there is the question of a journal my sis kept, that Sanchez said he held for me, should I ever come his way, as it was too expensive for him to mail the weight. He knew where it had been hidden in the barn, a woman's private thoughts, and retrieved it. To be truthful, I hate the thought of reading her writing, as I'm sure I'm mentioned with scorn.

My sis was a beautiful woman, inside and out, and as talented as she was beautiful. She was a writer, gaining the respect of the local newspaper in Illinois, before she married, as a ladies columnist.

Should some heathen Indian filet my heart someday, he'll find a good part of it was occupied by my sweet little sister.

The sixth of the louts I seek is the scum-suckin' bastard son-of-a-whore who hired the back-shooters to do the deed, or so Ignacio believes. That pecker head is a former Pennsylvania Colonel, or so it is said; a man who held the line at Gettysburg's fishhook, not far from where my brigade and I took our stand. He and I should share a warrior's bond, but we share nothing of the sort.

He's a man who's killing now for a much less noble purpose, only to increase the pile of gold he already hoards. He's the murderer of a fine young man, a beautiful and loving woman and mother—although her body was never found, believed by Sanchez to have been burned to ash—and two angelic innocents. All over three hundred twenty acres of homestead sagebrush and a mud bog of a spring, rank water not worth a tinker's damn, which only served to wet the throats of a few mangy Mexican cattle.

It was only by the grace of God and the protection of a thick stand of cattails lining the spring's trickle that Sanchez lived to tell the tale. Otherwise I'd have thought, as the law seems convinced of...or is willing to lie about...that the fire was fate, their deaths an act of God. It came as no surprise to me that the gracious God I occasionally beseech...I should say beseeched...was not at fault, as Sanchez confirmed.

It was more'n two months before I got word of the Colonel's dastardly deed.

Sanchez wrote his letter in a timely manner, but it lay gathering cobwebs in the Salmon, Idaho post office...a corner of the trading post...for more than a month, awaiting my infrequent visit down from high on the mountain.

I've spent a rough month since, here in the high country, mourning my kin, and another week working up the roiling boil that fuels the resolve now simmering in my twisted gut, and a half-day packing for a trip from which I'm sure I'll not return. And to be truthful, I don't much give a damn if I do.

Last night, for the first time in five weeks, I slept the sleep of the dead-to-the-world with no dreams of fire and screaming babies—it's funny how coming to terms with oneself, and one's fate, settles one's sleep. Now, knowing exactly what my task is to be, I'm resolved to see it through, hell or high water. And pure hell it should be.

This morning I've stepped lively for the first time in more'n a month. I've packed the mule, Jackson, named for a hard-headed colonel who sent us into hell's fire more than once. I sucked up his latigo extra tight, giving a knee to the belly of the old blow hard, and giving the latigo another hard pull at the same time, as it's to be a trail-pounding trip.

I've also saddled the buckskin, and we are all three about to say goodbye to the high-mountain home I've come to love—a cabin where I've spent a half-dozen years trapping, skinning, and tanning, when not sawing and hammering, as if I was going to live another half century beyond my thirty years.

The place ain't much in the way of homesteader's improvements: lodge pole logs fitted and chinked with mud and dry meadow grass, a sod roof growing green with grass and wildflowers so as from above it looks to be part of the meadow, rough sawn log floor, and glassless windows covered with rough but sturdy shutters. The privy is only a few steps from the door, and built with the same careless abandon. And there's a spring near at hand that runs warm year round and serves for kitchen water in the winter, if you don't mind a little whiff of sulfur. It makes life a mite easier when otherwise you'd be melting snow and ice.

The place has been home and kept the critters and weather at bay for a good long while and, excepting for my intrusion, is as beautiful a spot as God ever created. And I'm not totally alone. The lodgepole pine and puzzle bark trees host squirrels and a hundred varieties of feathered critters. Deer and elk often visit the meadow and stream. Even bighorn sheep look and lord down from the cliffs above. All of them are more welcome than the occasional griz or the marauding black bear, who drop in all too frequently. On great occasion, a wandering wolverine has proven to be more than a pest, extolling his reputation as the angry old man of the forest—more trouble per pound than a bucket of rattlesnakes.

Beyond the stumps of those timbers I used to build the place, the pines surround the cabin sides and rear and climb the gentle hill behind, and across a sweet grass meadow twenty paces in the front flows a brook filled with six-inch trout that fry up crisp as bar crackers after they swim in a pan deep in poppin' hot sowbelly leavins'. Beyond the crick the meadow fingers into a stand of puzzle bark ponderosa so thick and tall they make you want to sing the praises of the Lord every time you stare into their shadowy depths, or up into their dizzying heights—particularly this time of year, when the crick runs cold, clear, and high with tears of the melting white mountain sides. Yellow blossoms of arrow leaf balsam root pepper the voids where the sun kisses the fingers of green...but I shouldn't think on it as it will soften my resolve.

Still, I'll miss the screech of the hawk and eagle overhead, the raucous scathing cry of the crows, the bark of the whitetail buck, the honk of passing geese, and particularly the ringing cry of elk bugling in challenge from the depths of the copse of puzzle bark trees when the leaves turn gold and frost again teases the sweet grass.

In so many ways I hate to leave this spot as it brought me peace for a good long while, but I have a job of work to do. And that job's a damn sight more important than worldly possessions, the glory of God's earthly adornments...or even peace of mind and soul.

I doubt if I'm up to the full task at hand. Not the moral part, for I've got no problem with that or being judged by my maker for the effort. Although I've stopped the dropping to my knees and talking with Him before my nightly rest, just in case He tries talking me out of my trek.

Since reading that dreadful communiqué from Señor Sanchez, I put far more stock in the "eye for an eye" part of the Good Book than in the "turn the other cheek" part.

If there was ever a group of thunder-pot-stains that need killing, it's this half-dozen and I don't believe an ounce of remorse will enter into the doing of it...presuming Ignacio Sanchez proves to be the truthful a man I believe him to be.

The hell of it is, I'm a little long in the tooth and stove up to be on the prod against this kind of odds. Even thirty years of living can be too much if the road getting there was sufficiently rough. The war and reb cannons did some damage to my parts, leaving me with a gimp in my hind leg and kink or two deep in my head-bone—it seems my temper refuses to be turned low once the blaze is lit, and it's oft times caused consternation, and worse, to those nearby when I've been riled. Dishonestly, in particular, turns my insides to storm. It's one of the reasons I've chosen the high lonely as a place to reside.

Nightmares of my sis and nieces have replaced the bad dreams of the war. I'd learned to think of my two nieces playing a game of jacks, so as not to think of the war. Now, the murderin' back-shooters have taken that pleasure from me. I bought the girls some nickel-plated jacks and a bouncy ball of Goodyear rubber, but never had the heart to deliver them, although I tried to bring myself to do so one time more'n a year ago, the only time I met Señor Ignacio Sanchez.

How-some-ever this visit works out, even gimpy as I am, my killin' skills are well-tuned, as I still roam the high lonely and keep my smokehouse hanging full and my beaver hoops stretched taut with fresh hides. I'm sure as-the-devil-is-evil not as fast as I once was, thanks to those miniballs and a near cannon strike, but I'm a damn sight more deliberate, and the lead I let fly most oft smacks meat. But even if I don't finish the job, God willin', I'll put a few of 'em toes up and on their way to meet old Satan before the rest of them get onto who's doggin' their trail and ventilating their ugly hides.

It's my hope that thinking "It's that McBain again," in the black of night will cause them great consternation before they die, and that they'll die hard and slow while crying for redemption and forgiveness. It gives me peace and pleasure to think on it.

I have the regrettable advantage of them not knowing of me or of my existence unless Sanchez let it be known. Regrettable for I was not claimed by my sister, due to the more regrettable fact I left her and our mother when I went off to do President Lincoln's work, and was so gut-twisted and anger prone by the experience when the work was done I thought them better off without me. When I finally got the blood off my hands, or at least somewhat out of my dreams, it was too late to return and mend my friendship with my ma and sis. For it had come to me from a good friend that while I was taken with the war my ma went to meet her maker and my sis had sidled up beside a good man. And I knew him to be, as he was a good friend from my childhood. And they'd gone west.

She had sidled up with my former good friend, Jacob MacIntosh, whom I'd always admired and respected—but a man who later had good reason to hate me, as many did—for it was his brother and my sister's intended I'd killed when only fifteen. But I knew in my own cold heart that Jacob would do well by my sis—he was not his brother's sort. His brother was the Cain of the biblical story.

And I knew my sister Sarah must have a great love for Jacob, as she left what she loved most, writing, to take up with him for a trek into the wilderness.

It was thoughts of my sis that brought me way out here among the Snake Indians in the high lonely, even though I never had the audacity to make myself known to her, and now it's too late to do so. Exceptin' for the trading post in Salmon, and a to a few Snake red men I've come across, the fact is I haven't made myself known to anyone.

I'm known by most I do now know as McBain,

by those I fought through the troubles with as Cap, and by the few I've called friend as Mac; and no man, except for the Army paymaster, calls me by my given name, Rufus, which I would much prefer to forget. And fewer yet know my middle name, Taggart, although I favor it.

Many, God willin' and the creek don't rise, will come to know, and rue, the name McBain.

## Chapter Two

ANGEL SANCHEZ and his younger brother Ignacio, named after his father, stood with heads bowed, hats in hand, staring down at the grave of their murdered father as the old priest said a final prayer.

"*Vaya con Dios*," Angel muttered, then turned and strode away, without even a thank you to the priest, his fifteen-year-old brother having to trot along behind.

"We go south now, Angel?" the youngster asked.

"No. I have things to do first," Angel replied, without looking back.

"Papa would say you're being hot headed, Angel."

"Papa has nothing more to say, Iggy," the older boy admonished. "Papa is with his God."

"His God?" the younger boy questioned as they neared the horse they'd inherited from their father.

"His God, not mine. Mine would not have let the gringos shoot down a good man like papa."

Angel slipped the slightly beat up single shot .43 Spanish Remington rolling block from the scabbard on his father's saddle, opened the breach and checked to see that it was loaded.

"*Qué pasa?*" the younger Sanchez asked, apprehensively.

"I go to the saloon, to ask questions," Angel said.

"Papa would not—"

"You go back to Señor Henderson's, Iggy, and care for the sheep. When I am satisfied, I will be along."

"They will shoot you down like a coyote, Angel," Iggy said, the concern in his voice.

"If they do, you go back to Arizona and join mama and your brothers. Nevada will be no place for you."

"*Por favor*, do not go to the saloon. The gringos…"

"I am only going to ask questions." Angel swung up into the saddle and eyed his younger brother coldly. "Go back to Señor Henderson's and mind the sheep. He only let us off to come to the funeral. He expects you back—"

"He expects us both back, Angel."

"After I find out how this happened to papa. You and I both know, papa was no thief, no *bandito*."

"The sheriff told you not to...how did he say... not to stick your nose into his business."

"The sheriff is just another gringo. And the death of our *padre* is my business. Go, now."

The younger Sanchez watched as his brother spun the dun horse and rode toward town, then turned and trotted away. It was twenty miles back to the Henderson ranch, and he had a long journey. As it was, it would be well after dark before he arrived.

He had lost his father, and he now worried that he'd never see his older brother again. Not only the sheriff, but none of the gringos liked the Mexicans or Chinese asking too many questions.

I've been at it hammer and tongs since before sunup, having made up my mind that six evil men will come to rue the day they met McBain.

"Stand still, you old fool," I say to my buckskin, Dusty, as I suck up the latigo after he's had a spell to get settled, and let out the bellyful of air he sucked in to try and trick me with its tautness.

Dusty's one of the finest mounts I've had the pleasure to work with, and I've worked plenty. He's surefooted and quick as a cougar, long winded as a bone-rattlin' winter norther, and steady as an anvil when trouble comes our way. Actually, he's not so old, still shy of ten, and tough as wang leather as he'd have to be to stay whole and healthy up here in the high country where I hunt and run a pair of trap lines to keep body and soul together.

Dusty was the third mount I was assigned by the U.S. Army, and I was able to buy him and the McClellan saddle he still carries for a pittance when the affair ended, as he too carries his share of scars. The mule, Jackson, tied next to him is a fine animal as well, if as hard headed as his namesake. He's black as a foot up a bull's butt, except for the small white blaze on his Roman nose.

So, no matter what comes, I'm atop good horse-flesh and leading a pack animal up to any task. What few possessions I've collected—besides the traps and my weaponry—and I've never needed much, are still in the two window, one door log cabin I'm leaving behind. My last act is the note tacked to the plank door.

> *To whosoever finds this note.*
> *Help yourself, neighbor, as I'm not returning.*
> *Take some, leave some for the next pilgrim.*
> *Please leave the bible, as*
> *it's bound to be consolation*
> *to the next wandering soul, and has long*
> *been the heart of this humble abode.*

Old Jackson the mule is packed with flour, salt, coffee, five pounds of dried beans, a satchel of dried red peppers, one fresh back strap of elk, and the dried meat of a tender whitetail. A sheep gut holds a half-gallon of water, to which I've added two handfuls of beans and a pinch of peppers, so they'll be soft enough to cook when I'm hankerin' for something to both warm up and clean out my insides. There's also a pound or more of last seasons dried berries—chokecherries and huckleberries—which is a luxury I allow myself upon occasion. I'm also fond of hard candy, but it has begun to pain my back chompers a mite, and I've had to stop stocking up on it on my bi-annual trips into town. The only item that might suffer from a fall on the trail is a quart of Old Diamondback whiskey, which I keep, of course, for snakebite treatment...and I surely think that a hard day on the trail is as serious as a snakebite.

The only luxury I carry is a travel book, *Innocents Abroad*, by a new writer, Mr. Mark Twain, a bit of a humorist who has brought me to smile a time or two. I was able to pick up a used copy, only slightly dog-eared, the last time I visited the trading post. It will help pass the time and keep my mind busy so I don't crazy myself with the thoughts of screaming children.

Most of the weight in the panniers is taken up by a pair of bear traps, only a little over forty pounds apiece, since I left the chain behind. What I might decide to trap on this trip probably won't have to drag the weight, as it'll take the worthless piker's leg in half. And there's my weaponry and accoutrements.

The 45-90 Sharps hasn't been fired in over two years, only hauled out when I was bothered by an old griz who took umbrage at my taking up residence in the canyon he seemed to frequent. He blessed me with a fine silvertip coat, calf-length, which I brought along just in case this task takes me into the cold months, and it makes a fine sleeping pad nonetheless. There's a triple handful of brass needing reloading, and I have the lead, powder, primers, and molds to do so. It'll give me a way to wile away the nights while on my way south. In a pair of saddle holsters flanking my horn there's two fine LeMat pistols, nicely converted from cap and ball to cartridge, which I took off a reb colonel at Gettysburg—a gentlemen who had no more need of them. The LeMat carries nine .30 caliber rounds in its spinner, and by rotating the firing pin on the hammer, fires a .63 caliber scattergun lower barrel which receives a 20 gauge shotgun shell nicely, a fine weapon for close work. My brass shot shells are loaded with cut up square nails. In my saddle sling is a shiny new Winchester 73, and on my hip is a 44 Colts Army Model also converted to cartridge, not as new as the Winchester, but a good deal more experienced. And packed in the bedroll behind my saddle is a two-shot 44 caliber belly gun fit for the most sneaky pleasure-house gambler.

I'm a squad of shootists on the hoof. In addition, and something I seldom carry but has an accompanying trimmed-to-length scabbard should the carrying become wishful, is a Boyle and Gamble saber-bayonet taken from a reb captain, originally with a 21" blade length but broken when I was attempting to pry a mount off'n my leg after it had been shot dead at Gettysburg and fell pinning me to the battlefield. I re-sharpened the blades remaining 12" of length and it now serves as a fine camp knife, long enough to chop kindling and sharp enough to shave with. It would, of course, serve to skewer a man, should it become necessary, and its hand guard makes a fine pair of brass knuckles, should close fighting call for such.

I'm carrying the firepower of a damn nigh a full company of single-shot-muzzle-loading rebs.

As I swing up into the saddle I grunt with the pain of my bum knee fittin' to horse, and Ranger, my old dog, finally looks up from his snooze, gets to his feet, stretches his 140 pounds of half-Irish wolfhound, half-Great Pyrenees, yawning prodigiously at the same time.

"It's gonna be a hard run, old dog. You might think about a'sittin' this one out. There's plenty of fat rabbits to hold you till some other old fool comes along and takes you to partner up with him."

Ranger cocks his shaggy head to one side, eyes me, then gives me a grumble of a yelp and leaps down off the porch, as if to say he's game for anywhere I'm man enough to lead him, and I have no doubt as he has been game for the four years since his old master died and he partnered up with me. He's often proved to be the only friend a man needs up here in the high country, running more than one griz or pack of wolves away from where I lay my head for the night—you'd think his 140 pounds was all sour bile and fangs when he gets his back up. He don't bark or growl much, and when he does you know there's a passel of trouble on the way. He, too, has trouble getting the devil out once his back's up. In that we're a pair to draw to.

Old Sweeney Tucker, Ranger's former master, rode into my camp slumped over the saddle and hot as a mink in mating season, with a load of furs and traps on the two mules he led. He proved to be sick as a poisoned pup, and I cared for him for most of a month afore his lungs filled and he gave up the ghost.

Ranger lay on his grave for most of a week without eating, growling whenever I came within a dozen steps, until I thought he'd starve there. It was only a haunch of venison that got him back on the trail, and ready to make friends with me.

Sweeney had two hundred forty dollars in gold in his poke, which, at his last request, along with the proceeds from the sale of his furs, mules, tack and folderol, I wired to the last known address of his family, after taking out a half dollar for a bottle of good Irish whiskey—at his suggestion—and a dollar for the cost of the telegraph. The old mountain man bequeathed me the dog, his horse…later et by a griz after being left in the corral while Ranger and I were out with Dusty running a trap line; Jackson, and Sweeney's two mules wisely jumped the fence and ran off for a while. Jackson returned alone, and the two mules moved on to greener pastures. He also left me two dozen smaller traps, and the two prodigious bear traps that make up most of the load in Jackson's panniers.

Well, I've thought on it long enough. It's gonna be a long row to hoe before I get where I'm a'goin', and then a hard row of stumps to uproot when I get there. I pray, for my sis's sake that I'm up to the chore.

I gig the buckskin, leading the mule away from the cabin without looking back. I've left my bible behind, and a good part of what it represents, tipping my hat at Sweeney's grave as I pass. Ranger decides he knows the way better than I, and takes up the point. I wish I could train him to lead this hard-headed mule, but that's a bit much to ask. Besides, once we get down into open country, well away from the lean-to shed he calls home, the mule won't have to be led. He'll take up our pace and stay along as if he was half dog himself.

So it's goodbye to the Salmon River and the Selway, and hello to the sage-covered desert country north of Nemesis, Nevada...after a week or more of hard butt-busting trail, some of which crosses lava flows that could pass for the hubs of hell, and if you make that, it's the Snake that'll try and suck you into her bowel and hold you till you're as cold as she is afore she spits you up blue and pink and green with moss and good for nothin' but fish food.

It'll be blood and guts from there on out, and—if the good Lord is paying any attention after I abandoned his good book—a lot of hurt followed shortly by a trip to hell for the half-dozen no-accounts from the Lazy Snake ranch. And more than likely, myself.

## Chapter Three

COLONEL MACE DILLON leaned far back in his ladder-back chair on his wide ranch house veranda and yelled through the open window, "Chang, bring us another bourbon and branch water."

"That's mighty hospitable of you, Colonel," the sheriff said, giving his host a smile, flashing a missing front tooth at him. The big barrel-shaped man rose and walked to the railing—remarkably light on his feet for a man of such bulk—then spit a long stream of chaw over into the dirt below, backhanded the spittle from his full handlebar mustache, and returned to the bench where he'd taken up residence while reporting the results of the inquest to the wealthy ranch owner.

"It's purely my pleasure, Tobias," Colonel Dillon said. "I appreciate your riding all the way out here to bring me the news...not that I was a bit worried about our position in this affair...not that we had any position or anything to worry about. Even though we were the only ones who had an ax to grind with that hard-headed Jake MacIntosh." The Colonel rose, unfolding long and lanky but standing with military bearing, then he relaxed, spreading his arms wide and yawning. "Up with the sun, you know."

"I'd best be going, Colonel," Sheriff Wentworth said, thinking he was taking the colonel's obvious hint, grabbing up his wide-brimmed hat and holding it in front of himself, deferentially.

"Hogwash, Tobias. You're staying for supper, then you can bunk with the boys." The sheriff's face fell, as if he expected to be invited to stay in the big house, but he kept the feeling to himself.

The Colonel placed a long-boned hand on the sheriff's shoulder. "I'm pleased our name didn't come up in this sad affair at the MacIntosh ranch, and I know that fact was partly your doing." The colonel smoothed chop sideburns, only now beginning to go gray, then smiled again and offered, "Chang has a fine rib roast that's been turning on the spit for an hour. I keep a few head corralled and corn feed them just for extra special guests like yourself. This roast will melt in your mouth."

Tobias grinned widely as the Colonel greased his

ego, and Dillon thought, *what a damn fool*, but continued, slapping the big sheriff on the back. "I want you to take a hindquarter back to town with you in the morning. We'll loan you a pack horse and you just turn him out when you reach home. He'll come back to his pards soon enough."

"As you wish, Colonel," the sheriff said, reaching into the open window for the drinks Dillon's houseboy was offering. He handed one to his host. "That's more than kind of you." The sheriff paused a moment, then added, "I see you've already moved some stock up the canyon onto the Bar M."

The older man's eyes narrowed until his salt and pepper, bushy brows almost touched. "Well, Tobias, you know our boundary is not fenced. If a few Lazy Snake head have wandered over there...."

"It's of little matter, Colonel. I suppose you'll own the MacIntosh place soon enough."

"Soon enough, Tobias, soon enough, sure as Sherman took Georgia." The colonel laughed, then changed the subject as the less attention called to the fact he would be bidding—the only bidder if he had anything to say about it, and he did—at the sheriff's sale of the Bar M. To the best of anyone's knowledge, the MacIntoshes had no relatives, and had died intestate. "Let's retire to the drawing room until the table's ready. How's Judge Thorne?"

"He asked about you, Colonel, and sends his

regards. Said he hopes you're satisfied with the inquest and his ruling."

"Fact is, you might take Felix a loin when you return. And tell him I appreciate his fine and fair jurisprudence."

"My pleasure, sir," the big sheriff said, but thought *a loin for the judge, and I get the hindmost.*

The sheriff followed the stockman into his drawing room, where the only snooker table in northern Nevada Territory resided, at least this side of Washoe Meadows.

Colonel Mace Dillon walked to the window and looked out over his spread, where a thousand steers were getting fat and a thousand yearling heifers were growing into fine breed stock—he'd again been blessed with a good grass year—and two thousand cows had bellies swelling with another batch for next year to grow his herd, and fortune, even more. And now he had room, and water, for two to three hundred more cows and calves.

And soon they'd be as fine a herd as there was in North America.

He'd gone east in the spring and bought a fine Aberdeen Angus bull—General Napoleon he'd been named by his Scottish breeder Ian MacTavish, in a moment of whimsy. He was raised then sold in Pennsylvania. Colonel Dillon had paid over five thousand dollars for the bull, long of loin and broad in shoulder and hip, the finest of his breed. And he'd hired a man, a caretaker, to personally accompany the animal on a train, outfitted with a special stock car that should be arriving within the month. Year after next, the northern Nevada desert should be dotted with fat long-loined heifers that would bring the highest price in Chicago.

Things were coming along just fine.

Just fine.

There was nothing to stand in the way of acquiring another several thousand acres of good grass and water on up the canyon, now that the MacIntosh bunch were out of his hair.

He had a couple more spreads to buy, or purloin, as he had the Bar M, and he'd own all the water in the valley, and have room for five thousand head. In northern Nevada every gallon of spring water was nearly worth its weight in gold to a stockman.

But one year, and one ranch at a time.

He'd buy them all out at a fair price if he could… if not, then devil take the hindmost.

And time was on his side.

We'd picked our way south for three days when we hit the hell-on-earth country not crossable by wagon, and barely by horseback. Nothing is harder on the feet of a hoofed animal than old lava flows— and it's no less hard on those of us, Ranger and myself, with softer tissue. I normally wore moccasins, traded from a Snake squaw, but took to wearing my hard knee-highs, scarred with many a battle, when we came upon the lava.

It's as if the devil his worthless self designed the country to kill man and horse—not only was the country knife edged, a million razor sharp stone edges, but it was virtually without grass for the animals and nary an animal lived in its nooks and crannies to feed a hungry hunter, man or dog. Just as you think the riding is easy along a highway of glassy lava, a smooth-topped flow will suddenly be breeched by a four or five or more foot deep chasm, too wide to jump, with bottom peppered with jagged chunks of lava that would discourage a lizards crossing, much less a horse or mule. Only the buzzards circling above traveled with impunity, and even then there was not a tree to rest a weary flyer.

The black hubs-of-hell was a field of traps, holes waiting to snap the leg of man or beast, and jagged edges that would slice through canvas pants and peel flesh from bone in a careless heartbeat. By the time we ended the first day of hunt-and-peck a foothold, and found a sandy bed under an outcropping so dog and I didn't have to sleep on sharp shards, the horses' and mules' hocks were sliced and bleeding, and I had to wrap Ranger's soft feet with pieces torn from the tail of my extra Lindsey Woolsey shirt.

What I estimated to be about halfway across, we came face to face with a band of twenty or more Shoshone—commonly known in the east as Snakes—who rode up out of a deep cut in the lava, and reined up not a hundred paces from where I'd jerked rein. Had I heeded the neighing of Dusty, I'd have been forewarned and able to avoid the confrontation.

Three braves approached to within fifty yards as I filled my hands, each with a LeMat, even those sixteen shots of 30 caliber—I always keep the cylinders under the firing pin empty as I've seen more than one pilgrim meet his maker from dropping his own weapon—and two twenty gauge shotgun shells would not be enough for this large band even if each was a killing shot...not a likely result in a running battle, as that was what it would be, should they start filling the dry air with lead. And the running, in this pile of razors, might be as damaging as flying lead.

As luck would have it, one of the three braves was Knows-No-Horse, with whom I'd once shared a roasted grouse when he'd stumbled into my high lonely camp, alone, afoot, and hungry. He recognized me, and called the others off with gibberish I didn't understand, before a ruckus began—a ruckus that would surely steal me from finishing my task as it would be hard to do while staked out in the hot sun sans my fine head of hair, while the crows picked at my eyes.

They rode on with a peaceful wave, and I paused a moment to thank the God with whom I've had little conversation of late.

It took four days to cross lava hell, two more than I'd expected, and our goat guts of water were bone dry by the time we reached the towering edges of the Snake River gorge.

On the seventh day after a swim across the wide river that nearly took us all to meet our maker, I pulled up on a low rise amid sagebrush, looking down on the long ribbon of steel that was the Transcontinental, and row of poles that I knew carried the wire and Mr. Morse's code.

And I know that somewhere just a few miles to the east is Nemesis, and there it begins.

## Chapter Four

ANGEL SANCHEZ LAY face down on the cold stone floor of the Nemesis jail. He'd been there for well over a week, regained consciousness there after being beaten senseless when he'd confronted Sheriff Wentworth in Sally's saloon about the killing of his father. For the third time since his incarceration, he'd been knocked senseless. This time, as he awoke, he decided that all he was doing with his sharp tongue was cutting his own throat. He slowly climbed to his feet, then stumbled to the nearby bunk and collapsed prone.

"When you gonna get it in that chili-soaked brain of your'n?" Stubby, the Sheriff's deputy, called from across the room where he leaned back in the Sheriff's chair, his feet on the desk, a large stogie shoved in his mouth, the local weekly paper in hand.

"Get what?" Angel asked, without rising or even lifting his throbbing head.

"You can't sass the Sheriff, you dumb greaser."

"*Sí*," Angel said. "I will not do so again. Can I go home now, *señor*?"

"No, you can't go home now. You've got to wait until Judge Thorne makes his rounds through here… then I'll be surprised if they don't haul you off to the territorial prison, threatening a saloon full of city folk like you did with that Remington."

"*Puercos*," Angel said under his breath, referring to those who'd been in the saloon as pigs.

"What?" Stubby asked.

"*Por favor*, where is my rifle, Stubby?"

"You can call me Mr. Stubby."

"*Señor* Stubby…where's my rifle?"

"Doubt if it's still yours, but it's here in the rack."

"And this gringo judge…when will he—"

"Damn you're a smart-ass whelp. It's Judge Thorne to you, and he'll be here when he's damn good and ready. The judge is a busy man, and friends with the governor and with President Ulysses S. Grant. But then you wooly bugger boys from Mexico wouldn't know nothin' about any of that."

"So, *señor*, when will President Grant's friend come to do court?"

"When he's a mind to. Now shut your pepper hole and let me read this paper."

Angel was no longer in a mood, nor a condition, to argue. Sleep, sleep was what he needed, and to get well, so he could get his rifle, and take his revenge.

I let Dusty pick his way east along the track, finally cresting a small rise with the setting sun at our backs. In the distance, where the track made a bend around a small mountain that in Idaho Territory would be called a hill, I could see the outline of roofs and some smoke rising from rooftops. Folks, I figured, were fixing the evening meals as it was too damn hot, even in May, for fires for warmth. The thought of food made my mouth water and my stomach complain.

I'd trimmed the green from the last of the elk loin just last night, and the rest of it had been so ripe that even with plenty of salt it wasn't fit to eat, so all day my stomach had been flapping from my belly button to my backbone, wondering if I'd forgotten that food was part of the process of living.

Still, I hated going into a strange town, a town probably full of men I'd have to kill, when I couldn't see into the shadows. Finally, feeling some disgust, I found a small ravine, its bottom lined with grass for the stock, where I could at least brew the last of my coffee—I'd filled my goat guts from some potholes I figured were in the bed of the catch-as-catch-can Humboldt River just yesterday. A place where I could build a smoldering fire without it calling attention to those on the two track trail that roughly followed the Transcontinental rails. I spread my bearskin coat, lay back, and scratched the old dog's ears. "Ranger, you stingy old hound, you kept that jackrabbit you caught all to yourself. Still and all, you keep the critters at bay whilst I catch some shut-eye, and I'll find you a bone big as a donkey's dingle on the morrow."

The dog lay his muzzle between his paws, content as he'd been well fed due to his own enterprise, and was asleep by his second breath.

"Fine damn camp guard dog you make," I mumbled, but I, too, faded in two heartbeats. My stomach would just have to do all the growlin' needed to protect the camp until the sun was well up.

But as always, I awoke well before the sun lined the mountains to the east. I downed a couple of mouthfuls of cold coffee from the pot, dumped the grounds, poured a little water for the dog from a goat gut, and packed up and saddled up, figuring on watering the horse and mule when I got to town. From almost a half mile away, I circled the little town, able to see down into it from the steep bank to the south.

The rough, mostly clapboard, town lay four blocks along the rails, all of the buildings except a water tower to feed the steam engines to the north of the rails as the hill rose steeply to the south. The little berg was only two blocks deep north to south, and that just along the secondary main drag, which seemed to be a road off into the ranch lands to the north. I'd bet the road along the rails would be named Front Street. From the hill, I counted a dozen or more buildings of some consequence, and half of them were false fronts. One seemed substantial, with a sign in gold announcing it to be the Mystic Palace, and a hotel—with two stories and a cupola it rose above the rest. A corral, divided into four smaller corrals, and a railroad stock loading ramp were the main feature of the east end of town. Nemesis, although it was on the Central Pacific section, looked to be almost as fleeting as many of the hell-on-wheels towns that had sprung up along the Union Pacific as its portion of the Transcontinental marched westward.

Gambling, pleasure ladies, and whiskey were the mainstays of those towns, and most of them didn't last as the road moved on west. But Nemesis, built on the Central Pacific portion of the road, had, as a cinnabar—mercury—mine was discovered in the hills to the south, and enough water sprung from the earth to support substantial herds to the north, as was evidenced by the stock corrals.

Just to be on the safe side as I've always been a cautious soul, I staked the mule out in a deep meadow a mile to the south of town in the sage-brush, smoketree, and tamarisk hills, giving him the last of the water from the goat guts, hid my pack and some of my weapons in a cache in a small wind cave on a steep hillside, and only then made my way into town from the east, as if I'd been following the rails west...just another California-bound pilgrim who couldn't afford the cost of a train ticket.

No one paid me much attention as I came to Paradise Street, which was the road running out of town to the north, and where a half-dozen of the primary buildings of the town rose. I'd been wrong about the street along the rails, it was named Dillon Street. One of the structures, on the west side of the street, I noticed, was the Sheriff's office, clapboard in the front and stone in the rear, which I presumed was the jail. Only two doors down, past a tonsorial parlor separating the two, was Sally's Salacious Parlor of Fine Food and Folderol. As serious as my mission was, I had to smile at that one. The place's sign stretched all the way across its twenty foot wide façade, and the letters were small as saloon signs go.

Dusty was happy to be tied where he could nose

through the moss and bury his muzzle in water trough, and drew deeply on it.

Salaciousness was not on my menu, but food was. I was pleased to see upon pushing my way through the swinging saloon doors that breakfast was being served. Ranger, in his normal way, followed me inside. I was not surprised to see that the front was false and the saloon itself had a canvas tent for a roof over clapboard side walls and a rough sawn floor. At that, it held a long fancy dark-paneled back bar with carved gargoyles glaring down at the customers, a reclining scantily-clad lady of the evening in oil paint over shelves lined with liquid imbibement, and a dozen round tables with ladder back chairs peppered the place, tables I was sure would fill with town folks, gamblers, drovers, field hands, miners, railroad men and stockmen, come afternoon or at least evening.

Now only four other patrons enjoyed the fare. I took a seat in a ladder back chair, one of many, near a front window made up of several dozen small panes of fine clear glass and laid the 45-90 at my feet on the floor while Ranger flopped down beneath the table. I nodded in a friendly manner to the bartender, a man with garters on his sleeves and his clamp-on collar askew, who was wiping down the bar. He had a waistcoat unbuttoned and only held together by a watch fob and chain. I noted the hook at the end of the bar where a cut-away coat hung. He, had he been buttoned and collared, and could be ready to go to a St. Louis opera house to enjoy Jenny Lind. He ignored me; obviously I was hiding my hunger well, and maybe didn't suit his taste in attire.

Finally, a young woman, stick thin with a prodigiously long swan-like neck, dressed, to my surprise, more like a house maid than a soiled dove, made her way out of another swinging door separating the front room from where I surmised was a hallway to a kitchen out back, separated from the main structure to keep the fires safely away, but with a row of cribs lining the hallway between for "salacious" pursuits. It would have been typical for a pleasure and gambling house in a hell-on-wheels town.

She carried a thirty-cup gray graniteware coffee pot, almost more than she could handle, and filled some tin mugs on her way to where I'd put my back to the clapboard wall.

"You eatin' or just restin'?" she asked, with a tired smile.

"Like to be eatin', if you recommend the fare."

"I do, but then I'm paid to," she laughed, and I decided I liked her.

"That's a big dog," she said, looking a little apprehensive.

"And he's got a big heart, to those who'll give him a scratch on the ears."

She reached under the table and did so, and Ranger allowed it, even giving her hand a lick.

"So if a fellow was to be wolf hungry?"

"The flapjacks are hard to beat...plate big and filling."

"Do that, and a pile of sowbelly and two or three cackle berries if the cook has some fresh ones... basted if he has the sowbelly."

"You want coffee, and maybe a shot of who-hit-john to sweeten it?"

"Sound's like you know the wants of a man who's been long at the saddle." I gave her my best toothy grin.

"Too damn well I do," she said, and said it was if she meant it. It wasn't often I heard a lady swear, but it didn't sound offensive coming from her.

I laughed. "So, you work nights as well?" I figured I could be a little forward, as the sign did say "salacious."

"Used to," she said with a coy smile, "but the Colonel shut down the cribs, said it wasn't Christian-like and if we were to become an honest town, we had to hold our heads high. Still, a fella could find me after hours...."

"Ain't that something," I said. "Coffee please," I requested, but she was already filling a cup she'd had dangling from a finger as she'd had to carry the pot with both hands.

"Is this Dillon of a Mormon persuasion?"

"No, sir.   Since the Mormon war and Sierra Nevada becoming a state, the Mormons don't hold much sway hereabouts."

"So this Dillon is such a moral sort he can't abide by pleasure ladies?"

She laughed, at little sarcastically I thought, at that.  "I guess some would think he's a moral sort, and I wouldn't disclose it if'n he weren't," she said, then returned to business.   "Enrique, the cook, makes a mean salsa, which comes with the eggs should you have an iron digestive tract."

"I'll give it a try...always did have more courage than good sense."

She laughed as she headed back toward the doorway in the rear, again pouring coffee as she went.  The coffee, I quickly discovered, was hot as Hades and strong enough to float a spoon.

As I saucered and blew it to cool it, through the glass I watched a man in a cutaway coat—the town seemed to be taken with fancy dress—approach the most substantial single-story building in town, the Stockman's and Merchant's Bank, across Paradise Street from the saloon. As he approached the doors he pulled a large key ring from his belt and opened the bank's double doors.   It was the only brick building I'd noticed, and was built as if someone thought the town would last. He disappeared inside.

Just as I got the coffee cool enough to sip, a horse-backer reined up beside where I'd tied Dusty just outside the saloon door. He dismounted, pulled a lever action from its saddle scabbard, then meandered over next to the bat-wing doors of the saloon. But rather than enter, he just leaned up against the wall and kept a look on the bank. I found it a little strange, as he seemed a nervous sort, and even more so when he pulled a hog leg from its belt holster and checked his loads.

About that time, another two hard-looking riders, in dusters even though it was already too warm for a light coat, reined up in front of the bank and dismounted. I thought for a moment they were heading across to the saloon, but they paused at the rear of their horses, and looked up and down the street, studying it carefully, before turning back and heading for the bank doors. Both of them hoisted their side arms, making sure they rode free and easy in the holster, and one toted a sawed-off double barrel scatter gun fit for a Wells Fargo coach, although he tried to keep it concealed beneath the duster.

I guess I've been down to many rough roads, for all of this shouted trouble to me with a capital "T." Even as much as I can't abide a dishonest man, one who'd take the hard-earned savings of those who grub their money from the land, or a hard rock mine, or even a merchandise counter a penny at a time, I decided then and there to stay the hell out of it; then the dumb ninny who'd leaned on the wall next to the bar doors, the lookout I presume, walked over and steadied his rifle across the saddle of my horse. Damned if I was going to see Dusty shot being a leaning post and a barricade for some owlhoot of a scrubby looking outlaw.

I could hear Ranger's low growl coming from under the table. He didn't seem too much like the lay of things either, or maybe he'd just noted the knotted clamp of my jaw.

I rose just as the skinny girl appeared with my plate full of steaming flapjacks and eggs.

"Damn," I said, grabbing up my Sharps and jerking to my feet.

"You don't like the plate?" she said, looking startled.

"Get away from the doors and windows, and get down," I snapped at her, "There's trouble afoot," and her eyes grew as big as the plate she carried.

I moved to the doors just as the bank doors threw aside and, carrying a couple of sacks, the two hard-looking cobbers ran from the bank.

Pushing through the batwings, I brought the Sharps over my shoulder in a wide arc and caught the near bandit where his thick neck met his shoulder. He went to the ground under the heavy barrel like a sack of cow dung meant for the garden. As quickly as the big rifle's octagon barrel bounced off the old boy I kicked his rifle out into the street and shouldered mine, then had to hesitate as a fine looking woman, screaming at the top of her lungs, followed them out the double doors, only to be struck down by one of the bandits, wielding his heavy revolver. I adjusted my aim and fired at the nearest mounting bandit across the dusty road, who was clear of the woman. Unfortunately for his mount, he was standing in front of the bay he rode, and both of them went to the ground in a heap—too much rifle for close work.

The second rider, who may have killed the woman with his hard blow, fired both barrels of the scattergun in my direction, then slung the gun aside. The whole street reverberated with the blast; the window next to me blew away as if a mule had jumped through it. He managed to mount his sorrel, as I had to wait for him to be well clear of the woman, and jerked rein, giving his big horse his heels as he palmed his six shooter and let fly another lead pill in my direction.

I, too, had my Colt's in hand and stepped out away from the horses in front of the saloon, and lay down on the rider, pounding away down the dirt road leading north out of Nemesis. He had seventy-five paces on me before I got the first shot off, and did not flinch, but rather hunkered down, let another shot fly back my way, and pounded on. He was getting away, with a sack full of hard-earned still in hand. As quickly as I could load and hammer back, I fired two more times, to no effect.

I holstered the Colt's, noticing that his retreat plan had not been well thought out as he continued straightaway out of town on a road straight as a section of Transcontinental rail.

I dug another 45-90 cartridge from my pocket and reloaded the Sharps. Folks were starting to run from their places of business and from a couple of houses fronting on Paradise Road, then I remembered that the man I'd felled near the door had a sidearm, and it was a good thing I did. I swung on him just as he was coming to his senses and pulling his six shooter.

"Don't do it, pilgrim," I yelled, "or you'll be meeting St. Peter for lunch."

He threw the six gun out into the road, and went back to moaning over his shoulder.

Yelling, "Get back," I bellowed at the top of my lungs at those filling the dirt road, and dropped to one knee as the filling street quickly emptied. I took a deep breath, hoisted the heavy rifle, adjusted the top sight for three hundred yards, and waited another slow count of four until I figured he was that distance. Lost in the moment, I didn't even feel the rifle buck in my hands, but, confident, rose to my feet as I saw sack and sidearm fly from the retreating offender's hands, flung away as he pitched forward and dove from the saddle.

The sorrel pounded on unhurt, I'm happy to say.

"A hell of a shot." It was the bartender who'd ignored me.

"I've made longer," I said.

"But not more important to Nemesis," he said, a wide smile on his face. "I had two years worth of earnings in that bank."

I was concerned about the woman, a fine-looking sandy haired lady in a pink bustled dress that had St. Louis or Chicago or New York written all over it...but two other ladies were helping her to her feet and she looked to have her senses about her.

"Glad I could help," I said to the bartender. But my stomach turned, as I was sure I'd added two notches to my list of dead men, and it never sat well with me.

We turned back to the saloon, where three men were hoisting the first bandit to his feet. His arm dangled at his side, his shoulder obviously broken.

"You son of a bitch," he spat at me, "them was my brothers you shot down. Everette may be lying out there bleedin' out, and y'all are here shootin' the breeze."

"Just did what needed doin'," I said, taking no pleasure in the fact.

"You'll die hard for that," he said.

"Odds is," I said quietly, "we'll all die hard. This country's not much for dying easy."

"Shut up," the bartender said to him. "Lock him up," he barked at to those holding him. "See if those other two are alive enough to hang...then go out to the sheriff's ranch and tell him he's needed."

"You hang bank robbers here in Nemesis?" I asked.

"That's how she got her name. We don't abide robbers, rapists, and damn few Republicans, an' we sure as hell don't abide a man who'd strike a woman," he said, then laughed and pushed me toward the batwing doors. "Get on in there, you've got a fat steak and a bottle of Black Widow whiskey coming, friend. Town owes you and I owe you. The city council will have to talk about some kind of reward."

"Doing right is all the reward a man should ask for. How-some-ever I have worked up a bit of an appetite." I said it and was surprised by it, as killing should have soured my gullet. Fact was, it seemed to have made me even hungrier. Deep inside, and unsaid, I can only hope those bandits were some of the same who plied their evil on my sis, her husband, and her beautiful daughters—but I know that's a daydream.  Those scum suckin' pigs still breath God's good air, but I hope not for long.

"I've got to go check on Miss McGregor.  I'll be along in a moment."  He strode away to where the women were attending to the sandy-haired lady in the bustle.

As I made my way to the batwing doors, I couldn't help but realize that he'd called her Miss.  There were damn few single women between St. Louis and California, and women as fine looking as that one were rare as hair on a frog…but then what could I offer any woman, as the path I'd chosen will, I'm sure, lead me straight to hell.

I might as well go with a full stomach.

I had to clean the glass shards and mullion splinters off my table and chair before sitting.  The thin girl had removed my glass-peppered breakfast and had broom and dustpan in hand and was doing her best to clean up the mess.

"No one hurt in here?" I asked.

"No, thanks to you I'd run behind the bar, and the rest of the patrons were far enough away and under the tables with your warning, and they avoided the flying glass.  And the shot went into the wall…a new decoration for the patrons to jaw over."

"Good.  The bartender said something about buying me steak and eggs and a good bottle of whiskey."

"Sure enough," she said, and hustled to the back and out the door.

Looking at the size of the hole blown in the windows and the number of mullions blown away, it must have been a ten gauge loaded with cut up dimes or square nails. I was relishing the thought that I hadn't been the recipient of that load when the girl returned with a bottle of good whiskey, and to tell the truth, even though a little early for my taste, I was ready to clean the dust and taste of blood out of my gullet.

It had been quite an introduction to Nemesis, but I feared...or maybe hoped...the worst was yet to come.

## Chapter Five

AS I SHOVED in the last bite of a fine chunk of beef loin, the bartender pushed his way in through the batwings, strode across the floor covered with goober peanut shells and the remnants of glass shards, and joined me at the table.

"The sheriff wants you next door to give a statement."

I eyed him for a moment. "What for?" But I knew it was a dumb question. And he didn't reply, merely looked at me like it was as dumb a question as I knew it to be. I was merely vying for time; time to decide if I wanted to sit with some lawman after I'd just shot a couple of men down in his town, deserved lowlifes or not. I sighed deeply, then answered, "I guess that's understandable."

"I'm sure it won't take long. I noticed your rig,

the pair of LeMats in the saddle holsters, the Sharps you carried in. Are you a gun for hire, sir?"

I laughed at that, wondering if he would have thought I was an army for hire had he seen the belly gun, the lever action Winchester, and the bear traps I'd hidden in the wind cave. I smiled sheepishly, and offered, "Hell no, I can barely keep meat on the table."

He didn't smile. "Pardon me for saying so, but that's hogwash. I watched your style, Mr...?" He extended a hand. "I'm Paul Alexander Polking-horn...and you're?"

Hesitating a moment, I finally grasped his hand-shake, and lied, "I'm Taggart Slade." I quickly decided I shouldn't use the name McBain, since I knew my sister occasionally used her maiden name as middle, and I was a long way from wanting myself tied to the Bar M ranch...at least not yet.

"Like I said, sir, I believe you're a bit more of a shootist than you care to admit. All three of your pistol shots found your target. One in the shoulder of that retreating bank robber, one in his lower back, just a flesh wound on his side, but still a hit, and one in the buttocks. Had he lived, he would have been spending his long-in-the-tooth years standing. And your final rifle shot blew his spine away between the shoulder blades, I imagine taking a goodly part of his black heart with it. That was some kind of shooting,

Mr. Slade." He eyed me for a moment, awaiting a reply. Instead, I took another sip of the rather fine whiskey he'd provided, so he continued. "Slade...are you that lawman from down Texas way?"

I decided the less said the better, but I could hear the buzz across the saloon, which had filled up with townsfolk since the robbery, most of them eying me until I lifted my eyes to their stare, then they cut away. So I avoided the question. "I'm just a wandering pilgrim trying to find some peace."

"Those are LeMats on your saddle, are they not?"

"You've a good eye for weapons, Mr. Polkinghorn."

"So you were a Reb in the war?"

"You are a curious man, Mr. Polkinghorn."

"No offense meant," he said, holding up both hands, palm out.

"None taken, however I was a member of Mr. Lincoln's army, not that I care to remember any of the recent unpleasantries. Life, in my opinion, should gallop forward with the past forgotten...for the good of everyman in this saloon, and every state in this union."

"I agree," Polkinghorn said, again extending his hand. We shook again, then he offered, "I'll be happy to walk next door and introduce you to the sheriff."

I arose. "I'd be obliged, and I'm obliged for that fine meal." I picked up the bottle of Black Widow from the table, only three fingers light of full. "You did say a bottle?"

"I did," he said with another broad smile, and headed for the batwings. I followed, carrying the bottle with me and pausing to stuff it into Dusty's saddle bags before continuing.

I rubbed my chin whiskers, two weeks long, as I passed the tonsorial pallor. Maybe after my "statement" I could take the time to blow a quarter on a shave and a trim, particularly since barbershops are the gossip centers of most towns, and I was a man seeking information.

This time I instructed Ranger to flop down near the door on the boardwalk.

As Nemesis was also the county seat, it seemed the city marshal shared the space with the county sheriff, as there was a second desk in the room with a hand-carved name plate that said Sam Pritchard, City Marshal, but it was at the sheriff's desk where a large man with a handlebar mustache sat, eyeing, a little lasciviously, I thought, the same light-haired lady in the bustled gown who'd taken a hard blow to the head from the bandit who'd fired his scattergun at me. Her cheekbone was badly marked and already turning blue around a red-lined cut—but even that detracted little from how comely she was.

Eying me like a bull at a bastard calf, the sheriff did not bother to lift his prodigious bulk from the chair when we entered. I snatched my broad brimmed hat off, not in respect for his laziness but rather since a lady was in attendance.

Polkinghorn introduced us, calling out his full name, Tobias Stanford Wentworth, and I shook with the still-seated sheriff and nodded to the lady, who I learned was Miss Madeline McGregor. She did not seem to look upon me with pleasure, but rather like I was a pitcher of soured milk she'd pulled from the cooler when hoping to make a pudding. Her expression was curdled as well.

"Take a seat, Slade," the sheriff said, motioning me to a chair against the wall. His speech carried a hint of a whistle, I guess as a result of a missing front tooth, and his remaining teeth were stained tobacco brown. It took a second for it to soak in that I was Slade, a name new to me that I'd plucked out of the air. I did have a sergeant who served under me who was tough as horseshoe nails, and I admired him until he was shot through the brisket and died in less than a heartbeat.

Miss McGregor had a parchment in front of her, and a quill-tipped pen in hand. An inkwell and blotter were near.

"Miss McGregor is a teacher here in Nemesis, who of course has a fine hand, and has kindly agreed to put your statement on paper."

She had a small cut and angry welt on her cheek.

"I'm sorry you had to take that blow, ma'am," I offered.

"And I'm sorry you had to shoot down those men, particularly the one you shot in the back, four times or so I understand, who was no longer a threat to anyone."

I was so taken aback I merely stared at her.

"That's Miss McGregor's opinion, to which she's entitled," the sheriff said, to his credit I thought, particularly when he continued. "We're glad to get the folks' money back." He stuffed a little chaw in his cheek with a fat finger.

"I took no pleasure in it, however one of them did try to blow a hole in me through which you could drive a freight wagon, judging by the window it passed through."

The sheriff laughed, then sobered and said, "Let's get this statement out of the way. My wife's about to put a pullet in the frying pan."

I related the story just as it happened, with the exception of the fact that I claimed I'd ridden into Nemesis from the east, crossing the great salt flats… it was a good thing I'd ridden that country in the past, so as to make the story plausible.

When I finished, Miss Maddy McGregor arose and left without so much as a goodbye or go to hell.

After her bustle disappeared out the door, I turned to the big man, "Did you ask her if she thanked that ol' boy in the duster for the smack in the face he gave her?"

He looked a little dumbfounded, so I added, "She sure as hell didn't thank me for shooting down her attacker."

"No, she didn't. She's the preacher's daughter and he don't much take to violence either."

"Since when is self-defense a violence?"

"You'd have to ask Reverend McGregor that one." He eyed my Sharps, now leaning against the wall. "I should be asking you to leave your firearms in my care until Judge Thorne has a chance to review…."

My cold glare, and the fact I placed my hand on my sidearm, stopped him mid-sentence. I didn't give that comment the respect of a reply, and, although I could see the hair rise on the back of his neck, he didn't press it. I guess there's some value in folks, even sheriffs, knowing you can shoot, and are willing to do so if the situation calls for it.

The sheriff suggested, with the tone of a military order, that I hang around Nemesis until the circuit judge arrived and had a chance to review the statements. Which was fine, as Wentworth had no idea that I had no intention of leaving until my business in the nearby cattle country was complete, and there was a good chance I'd reside in the town's boot hill forever after, should my business culminate in the manner I figure it will.

I took my seat again and he, for the first time, arose. "That's it," he said, just as a voice rang out through an open door into the jail.

"You son of a bitch, you are gonna rot in hell."

I, too, arose and walked to the open doorway and peered inside. In a cell was the man I'd struck down with the heavy Sharps, his arm hanging loosely at his side. I had a tight smile when I replied.

"To be truthful, pard, I am not a bit sorry about your broke wing, particularly if it's the one leads to your gun hand. And I hope I don't have to rot in hell, 'cause I'll have to put up with you and your brothers burning next to me, and y'all don't seem fit company." I said it quietly.

He spat a gob into the corner of the cell, probably because I was too far to reach, then crossed the three steps to his stone bunk and carefully sat, grimacing, grasping his left shoulder with his right hand as he did so. Across the hall from him in another cell stood a Mexican boy, badly beaten and swollen, but adamant-eyed, staring through the bars. Enough condemning heat came from those eyes that I was surprised the bars didn't puddle to the floor.

"When do I see the doc?" the first man snapped.

"Mr. Hutchins," the sheriff called out, "I just hate to spend medical money on somebody who's bound to hang. But when the doc finishes with some deserving folks, he'll be along." He turned back to me. "We're through here," and I doffed my hat, turned, and headed for the boardwalk.

Next to the bank was a general store, and I was in need of supplies.

Behind the counter, shelving some tins of peaches, was a lanky fellow who could have been brother to the recent departed Abe Lincoln, but he was a mite better looking—which was not a difficult task—and wore a bushy mustache over his shaggy chin whiskers.

He obviously didn't hear me enter, was startled when I spoke up, and damn near fell off his step stool.

"You got any Arbuckle's?" I asked.

"Lord!" he said, stepping down. "You about saw me take a tumble. You move real quiet for a big fella." He eyed me carefully. "You're the fella who saved our bacon."

"Sir?"

"Shot down those highbinders who tried to make off with the town's money."

"Yes, sir, I'm that man, not that I took any pleasure in it. Now, you got any Arbuckle's? And maybe some dried beans, a side of fatback, and three cans of those peaches, if they don't come too proud."

He mounted the step stool again and snatched

down four cans, walked to a nearby shelf and got a large tin of Arbuckle's coffee beans, then turned to me, "Sugar? Salt? I got a new shipment of fresh chaw."

"Don't use the tobacco, but a pound of sugar and three pounds of salt would suit me fine." If I was fortunate enough to slay a deer, I might be able to salt enough meat to keep me for a long while.

He gathered it all together on the counter and I stood waiting for the total, thinking him a little presumptuous bringing four cans when I asked for three.

"You sure that's all?" he asked.

"Yes, sir, that'll last me, should I be able to down a rabbit or a fat deer out in the sagebrush."

He reached into a nearby jar and fished out a handful of hard candies, and into another fingered out at least a half pound of jerky.

As he was wrapping it all up in paper, I had to complain, "Sorry, friend, but I can't afford the luxuries."

"Yep, you can, friend. All this is on me, as a thank you for what you did for us."

I was only a little taken aback, but not so much I'd refuse. "Well, sir, that's mighty kind of you."

He extended a hand. "I'm John Pointer, slave to this counter here and mayor of Nemesis, and you're..."

"Taggart Slade." Again I lied about my name, and shook with him.

"You that lawman from Texas?" he asked.

I smiled. "I'm trying to leave my past behind me, Mr. Pointer." I didn't lie, I just didn't answer his question.

He cleared his voice. "We got a council meeting tomorrow...Saturday. Don't you be leaving as we may have a little reward for you, and something more to offer. Least ways if I have anything to say about it," he smiled, "and I damn sure do."

"Sir?"

"Just try and be close by come Saturday, or maybe we'll see you in church on Sunday? You are a church goin' man?" He didn't wait for my answer, but went on presuming it a yes. "Sunday would do just fine."

"I was headed for the barber from here, so it's likely you'll see me, least ways if the preacher goes easy on fresh-shaven newcomer sinners."

"New to sin, or just new to town?" Pointer laughed, and when I just smiled, continued. "I'll make sure he does go easy, either way. Not that Preacher McGregor pays much attention to anyone's opinion, other than the good Lord's."

"Is there a Chinaman in town?" I asked.

"Sure is. You need laundry done?"

"If it's church on Sunday. I got one shirt that

might suit, should it be scrubbed and have a hot iron taken to it."

"The last tent on the north on your way out of town headin' west...the one with a couple of tubs aside it.  I got a couple of ready-mades, but they come proud.  I'd give you one--"

I held out my hand, palm out, and he knew I meant for him to stop with the "I'll give you." However, if there was a reward to be had, I guess I can stand to be preached at...besides, could be that Miss Maddy McGregor, the preacher's daughter, would be over her mad by then, not that it would do me any good if'n she was.  Still, it might do a fella good to have a gander at a comely, God-fearing woman before he goes to meet his maker.

Gathering up my goods, I headed for the door, then paused a moment.  "Thanks, Mr. Pointer.  I'll pay my way next time in."

"I never thought you wouldn't," he said, and turned back to his shelving, yelling over his shoulder.  "You sure you can't use some tobacco? It's on the house as well."

I shook my head and waved over my shoulder as I headed out. I really hadn't yet asked anyone about what I came here to discover, and that was who had shot down my sister and her family.  I was saving that for the tonsorial parlor, and headed there after stowing my goods in Dusty's saddle bags.

## Chapter Six

---

"STAY WITH DUSTY," I instructed Ranger as I headed away toward the door next to the striped-painted barber's pole. He flopped down in the shade of the water trough. I was always a little surprised when the independent cuss obeyed.

Isaac Ironsmith was a Welshman, or so he said, and he said plenty, never stopping his chatter while he trimmed my hair, stropped his razor, worked up some foam in his cup of soap while my face soaked under a hot towel, and shaved me clean. He hadn't scraped razor against his own face in many years, as his white beard fell to mid-chest and, like the cobbler's son never has shoes, his white Moses-like head of hair hadn't seen scissors in a goodly long time. But his beard was trimmed and his mane of cotton white hair nicely combed, and he smelled of lilac, at least until you got breath-close to him.

All together it gave him a St. Nick sort of appearance, excepting for the fact he was rail thin. He did have a slightly bulbous nose—veined and cherry colored— sticking out through the white hair. I presume a result of seeing the bottom of many a whiskey bottle, which also explained the watery washed-out blue eyes full of red spider webs and the breath, rancid enough to melt candle wax.

"So," I asked when I was able to get a word in edgewise, "I heard you've had lots of killings here about?"

"Can't say as we've had more'n our share, 'cept for the city marshal, and the damn fool asked for it."

"How so?"

"He drew down on Shank Cavanaugh, same as suicide."

"And this Shank is who?"

"He's the *segundo*, the ramrod, not the cattle boss, that's Curly Stewart's handle...both of the Lazy Snake. Shank's a retired gun man, said to have killed a dozen men in fair fights 'til he got religion and went to cattle ranching with the Colonel."

"So, shootin' down the marshal was a fair fight?"

"Don't know that anybody drawing on Shank could be considered a fair fight, but, if it wasn't, I sure as hell wouldn't be the one to say so." I looked up at him as he'd stopped working the scissors, and he had fear in his flared eyes, the whites showing all the way around his pupils. "And you damn sure don't say I did."

"I damn sure won't," I said, with sincerity in my voice, then continued. "How about those folks killed out on some ranch nearby. Bar M, I think the place was called. I heard about that all the way up in the Salmon River country." I had to bite my tongue after saying it, as I'd advertised I'd come to Nemesis from the Great Salt Lake.

"Where's the Salmon?" he asked, not avoiding my question, but seemingly out of natural curiosity.

"North of the Snake. The Bar M?"

"Oh, hell, that was a fire, not a killin' like you're asking about."

I stayed silent a moment, then added, "That ain't the way I heard it. Man and his wife, and two children, shot down."

He seemed to think on that for a long moment, the longest he'd been shy of words since I walked in. Then, when I didn't speak, the silence got to him. "Well, a Mexican ranch hand had some wild story about a bunch of riders from the Lazy Snake, but the sheriff's investigation said that was all hogwash, a crazy Mexican's ranting and raving...to much sun. Wentworth was with the burial party and said there wasn't a gunshot in the lot of them.

Besides, the Lazy Snake is Colonel Dillon's place, and he's a good Christian man and the savoir of this town to boot. He don't hire no killers...'cept for Shank Cavanaugh, of course, but then he's come to Jesus."

"So, this Mexican, did he head back to the border?"

"Ignacio...no, he got himself shot down when he accosted some folks in the saloon."

"Sally's Salacious Parlor?"

"One and the same. So, tell me about this Salmon River country."

"Oh, hell, I haven't been there in years. Fact is, I came here from Mormon country, over near Salt Lake City."

"You got a half-dozen chubby wives, friend?"

I laughed. "Not even one. I suppose a sane woman wouldn't have me."

"A sane one has me, by the short hairs usually."

One quarter of a dollar and a five cent tip lighter in pocket, and smelling a bit like a lilac'd French whore myself, and I was out of there and pleased to be as my eyes had begun to burn and water from his kerosene breath.

It seemed one more stop at Sally's was in order.

This time I took a stool at the bar, a few stools away from four other dusty range riders. I used the beer foam towel hanging under the bar to brush away the hair from my shoulders and shirt until I got some notice.

Polkinghorn, the bartender, wiped his way down the bar to me. "Another shot of Black Widow?" he asked.

"Only if you'll take my dime. Pride won't let me keep this hand-out palm-up way of life."

"No problem, Mr. Slade."

"Thank you, Mr. Polkinghorn."

"Call me Paul, if you would and what should I call you?"

"Anything but late for supper," I said, trying to keep things light. "But Taggart if you like, or Tag is what my true friends seem to favor." I had to bite my tongue not to say Cap, as my mates in the Army called me, or Mac as later friends referred to me. With my new handle of Taggart and Slade, neither would make much sense. In fact, long ago during my childhood in Illinois I was called by my middle name, and it was often shortened to Tag, so neither was totally foreign to me.

As he was pouring my three fingers of Black Widow, I asked, "Barber tells me you had a shooting here in the saloon not long ago."

"Well, Tag, we've had our share," he said, "in addition to your little war this morning."

"This one involved some crazy Mexican... Sanchez, or something like that."

"And you're interested because?"

"Had an old friend, a cattle prodder I worked with back on the rail, way back in Nebraska, named Sanchez...who was a bit nuts...and was just wondering..."

"This ol' boy came up from Mexico, proddin' nothin' but stinkin' wooly sheep for a few years to get this far north. I knew him well, and he never said nothin' about proddin' cattle."

"Must be a different fella. So, how did this one get toes up under the daisies?"

"Who's this?" the deep voice rang out behind me. I should have sat in front of one of the mirrors behind the bar, so no one could slip up on me. I turned, slow and easy, on the barstool. He was tall, half a head taller than me, and had a face chiseled from slate and just as cold. His gun was worn butt forward on his left. He sported a cavalry shirt, striped trousers, and a hand-tooled cartridge belt on his waist, with enough cartridges to take on most of the town. The backs of his hands, resting on his waist, were scared, like he might have been a bull-whacker at one time, but he sure didn't look it now.

But his most noticeable feature were his eyes, the color of amber, a very distracting yellow, which contrasted with raven black hair and bushy black caterpillar fuzzy eyebrows. He sported a pencil thin mustache which only brought attention to bad teeth, which probably pained him and made him so disagreeable.

"Who wants to know?" I asked, although I suspected I knew as his fancy waistcoat, tooled leather belt and holster, and knee-high boots made him look like a gunfighter who wanted everyone to know his trade.

"I asked first, Mr. Smart Mouth."

I merely stared at him, wondering if his daddy was a snake and expecting any moment to see a forked tongue to go with the penetrating, unblinking, stare.

"No problem here, Mr. Cavanaugh," Polkinghorn said from over my shoulder. "Climb up here and let the house buy you a drink."

"In a second. Again, who the hell are you?"

"Taggart Slade, not that I'm sure it's any of your business."

"Anything happens in this town is my business, as I'm the man who watches out for Colonel Dillon's interests, and most of this town belongs to Colonel Dillon."

I was tempted to just kick him in the personals then beat the hell out of him while he was clutching his manhood, but I was not eager to have trouble as I had business to attend...and besides, with me seated on the high stool, and him standing not quite close enough, it would be a reach for a swing of the boot.

"So, who the hell is Taggart Slade?" His voice carried a tone of sarcasm that would anger the most forgiving parish priest, much less a fellow who'd just been hijacked of thirty cents by a barber whose breath would wilt your eyelashes.

Again, I merely stared.

He spat on the floor before speaking. "Look's like a pile of donkey dung to me." When that insult elicited no reply, he continued. "I hear you're a hell of a shot, at least when a man's riding away and you can back shoot him."

"Friend of your'n, was he?" I grinned, and the smile seemed disconcerting to him.

The silly grin and the question stopped him short, and he looked confused for a moment, then he growled and stepped just a little closer, just close enough, and lay his right hand across his belly on the butt of his six shooter.

I raised my hands high, as if in surrender, snapped my fingers, which distracted his gaze upward, then brought the boot up hard enough to change him from bass to soprano, burying it about ankle deep in his crotch. With a loud "oof," he stumbled backward, frog eyed and clutching his personals with both hands just as I suspected he might. Being a gunfighter as he was, a shot from a fella with raised hands from the toe of a boot was obviously unexpected.

Quick as the snake he looked like, I was on him, even though my bad leg almost gave out under me, driving a hard right with all my weight behind it, which broke his nose and caused him to reel back, his arms flailing. The nose was now a fire hose, spewing blood. I stayed with him, easily jerking his sixgun from its holster, flinging it over my shoulder in the direction of the bar. A driving left to his gut bent him and a right uppercut snapped his head back up just as the left came in again, splitting the tight flesh on his cheekbone, and he went to the floor to thrash among the goober peanut shells a little like a neck-wrung chicken. I let my boots do the rest of the work as he flopped and as I feared I'd busted my right hand, until I was dragged away by Polkinghorn and a couple of his customers.

Even with his reputation I was not surprised at my easy advantage as I've found a man who dresses and prances with the vanity of this one oft times so hates the taste and sight of his own blood that his knees fold under him. This man will hate to see himself in the mirror on the morrow, and will likely not show his face in public for a good long while. The next time I see him, he'll likely have firearm in hand and blood in his eye.

He lay gasping, alternately grabbing his personals and his nose, which was gushing blood, then his ribs that I'd kicked enough times and with enough force

—although it pained my bad leg something terrible to do so—so I knew he'd be breathing real shallow for a month or more. If I hadn't busted at least three of them, then my kicking's gone to hell in a hand basket.

Right now he was gasping, and I would imagine, wondering where the hell he was and where the freight wagon and six up had come from that had stomped him under. His eyes were still rolled back in his head.

"He'll kill you for that," Polkinghorn said, quietly, as they let me go.

"Not today," I said, and returned to the bar.

As I upended the rest of my drink, the batwing doors swung wide and a big barrel-chested fellow with a cutaway coat and expensive store-bought shirt, under a silk cravat and diamond stick pin, entered—and I could feel the hair on the back of my neck rise. He walked over to the heap on the floor, jingle bobs on his silver Spanish spurs ringing as he did so, and stared down at the man Polkinghorn had called Cavanaugh, and whom I presumed was the gunfighter the barber had referred to as Shank Cavanaugh.

Fancy-dan on the floor was still gurgling spit and blood, and was hardly the imposing sight the barber had led me to believe him to be.

The equally fancy barrel-chested man turned and

jingled over to the bar where I sat, and the muscles in my shoulders and neck knotted.

"You do that?" he asked. Seemingly amused, he stroked his handlebar mustache as he spoke, either a nervous habit or his own brand of vain, and continued to stroke it while he awaited my reply. My gut knotted along with my neck and shoulders and my mouth went dry, for I was sure I knew his identity.

"Took no pleasure in it," I said.

He extended a hand. "I'm Colonel Mace Dillon."

I shook with him, even though I was knotted up inside and wanting to shoot him in both knees to make him suffer hard before he joined Lucifer for a confab in hell.

"Taggart Slade," I managed. He had a black-smith's grip, and my hand already was paining me, maybe broken; it was all I could do not to wince, but then again you could have sawed my leg off with a cross-cut before I'd do so and let this man see me weak.

"You that lawman I heard about, shot down those thieves tried to rob my bank."

"I did shoot down some fellas who appeared to be helping themselves to the bank's money."

"A good deal of it my money, Mr. Slade, and the bank is mine as well. I'd like to buy you a drink."

"I'd be proud to accept, Colonel." I gave him as

kind an eye as I could muster, while I lied, and searched for a compliment, rather than pull my six shooter and put one in his gut. Instead I offered, "You and I were on the same field at Gettysburg, if you're that Colonel Dillon."

"I am, one and the same…and I presume you wore blue? Not that it matters a whit any longer."

"I did, sir."

"And your rank?"

"I was a captain, not that rank matters these days."

"Does to me," he said, then turned to the bartender, "Paul, sit us up with a bottle. The good stuff, not that panther piss you peddle to the others." Then he turned and spoke generally to those gathered in the saloon. "Take Shank over to the sawbones. Looks to me like he's having trouble catchin' his breath, and maybe you can get that ax-blade he calls a nose to stop bleeding…and maybe straight again. Looks busted to me, like a pile of stomped-on dog crap."

By the time he finished his instructions Polkinghorn had poured us, from a fancy cut glass decanter, each a tumbler full of fine looking whiskey about the same color as Shank's snake eyes.

"You looking for work?" the Colonel asked.

"Wasn't my intent," I said.

"Well, that's too bad, as we can always use a good man out at the Lazy Snake."

I downed my drink then offered, "Can I buy you one, Colonel?"

"That's Napoleon brandy, Mr. Slade. It's two dollars the shot, not a sum for the light of heart or purse."

I dug deep in a pocket, and pulled out a couple of twenty dollar gold pieces, my last, and dropped one on the bar. "We'll have two more," I instructed Polkinghorn, and he insulted me a little by testing the double eagle with a bite, then poured the drinks as I turned back to Dillon. "I've never been considered light of heart, Colonel. Occasionally light of purse, but never light of heart. In fact, I've oft times carried a heavy heart, and do so now. I hate shooting anyone, or," I nodded toward his man who was being lifted from the floor, still gurgling in his own blood, "having to beat a man senseless to try and beat some sense into him." I smiled a little sardonically, and added, "Ain't that just a hell of a note, having to beat a man senseless just to beat some sense into him?"

Dillon nodded and looked a bit surprised at my buying a drink, which was my intent, matching him drink for drink...at least for the short time I could. He had no idea that I thought it wouldn't do to be beholding to a man I planned to kill.

"Here's to Gettysburg," I said, and lifted my glass.

We downed our drinks, and I extended a hand again, shook, managed again to keep from wincing, and said, "Nice to meet you, Colonel." Then I strode out the batwings before I'd drunk up my total wealth, sucked up the latigo on Dusty, and reined away with Ranger at our heels to go find Jackson, the mule, and my other weapons.

The colonel had looked a little surprised as I left; obviously not a man used to having others walk away from him.

However, I had a sneakin' hunch I might be needing those weapons, and I was feeling the urge to clean them and check their loads.

And no urge to buy Colonel Mace Dillon anything other than a plain pine coffin.

## Chapter Seven

DILLON WATCHED THE MAN LEAVE. It wasn't often he was perplexed by another human being, and even less often a man walked away from him, particularly when he was buying him drinks in appreciation.

He turned to Polkinghorn. "What do you know about that fellow?"

"Not much. He came here from the barber, and you know Isaac, if there's anything to be pried out of a fella, he'd do so."

Dillon yelled at a man down the bar, one of the four who'd been there when he entered. "Stark, go next door and tell Ironsmith I want his company."

In moments the man referred to as Stark returned with the barber in tow.

After several drinks, Dillon had learned only that the man had ridden in from the east, and supposedly was heading west to California. Odd for a man with gold in his pocket that he wasn't riding the Transcontinental. Again he called Stark over.

"Go to the back and see if Lizzy is about. I need a pen and paper, then I want you to go over to the station and have Willard wire the sheriff in Salt Lake and see what he knows about this Taggart fellow."

"Yes, sir." He disappeared into the back of the saloon, where a door opened onto a hallway and another at the end led out to a free-standing kitchen where the place cooked for the customers. Beyond that was a small two story clapboard house, where the proprietor of Sally's resided.

I rode out of town to the west, stopping at the Chinaman's tent just long enough to pull my spare shirt and trousers from my saddlebags and arrange for them to be laundered and pressed, then crossed the tracks to the south near the water tower and a small wood yard and made my way into the hills. Mr. Wong Lee spoke passable English, and had three fine looking children, the oldest only waist high to him, with him only shoulder high to me, and a chubby little wife who never looked up from her steaming pot and washboard. He promised my shirt and spare trousers would look like new by tomorrow late, or I could pick them up with the sunrise on Sunday, and a tenth of a dollar would suit him fine.

Most that afternoon and evening I spent leading the mule around the hills looking for a place to call my own for a short while, and finally, three miles or so from Nemesis and well off the beaten track, I found a cave deep enough to hide my animals and myself, and a mite deeper which I had no desire to explore. One featured a trickle of water that would serve the four-footers and myself and keep us from the weather—rain, hail, or snow...which wasn't likely.

The cave was a little whiffy with bat guano when you wandered past the light flooding the opening from the setting sun, but was flat enough on the bone and hair ball littered floor—I was most likely usurping the home of some grumpy old black bear or mountain lion—to make a fine bed on my bear skin coat.

The mouth of the cave lay hidden by a thick hedge of tamarisk trees, which in turn was ringed by a hundred-pace-wide hedge of greasewood and sage; and should I want to stay hidden, which was likely, I'd be spending some time brushing away our tracks which led through the maze of chaparral to our lair. Had it not been for the foot-wide wet stream bed, mostly rocks and sand and only occasionally wet and less occasionally a drinkable size pothole, and that for a mere hundred yards, I'd never have found it.  And it took a bit of woodsmanship at that, having tracked and back-tacked some mourning dove and honey bees in their flights to and from the water, and some small game trails leading to and from same.  Some deadfall in the tamarisk copse served to enclose the mouth of the cave and as a makeshift combination corral and home was ready for man and beast before darkness set in.  Tamarisk is lousy firewood, but no oaks or pines were nearby, and I readily settled.

I would have to harvest some meadow grass should I leave the mule corralled there, then would have to employ some effort to clean up the place of his leavings should I sleep inside. But the weather was so fair I decided to sleep alongside the trickle under the stars. I tossed and turned with my hand and knee paining me, but even hurting in places, I was content in heart, knowing I'd already found the head of the viper.  Now to find the rest of the lowlifes.

As I lay back to enjoy the stars beginning to peek from the darkening sky, bats poured from the mouth of my new home.  No tellin' how deep the cave went into the mountain, but it turned out to be home to many thousands of flying bug eaters.

Up well before the sun, I took the lever action and climbed some higher onto the mountain, into the pinion pine, and was fortunate to jump a fat doe in short time, just below where some cedar breaks began.

I had her skinned and hanging from a tamarisk near camp before the sun's rays reached the bottom of the canyon where I'd taken up residence. More than half her flesh was stripped, salted, and drying in front of a low fire, and the rest sliced and saved for fresh. I rolled the fresh meat and bones, thinking in advance of Ranger's wants, and hung them up high out of critter reach.

Fresh fried liver and bacon was a treat almost as good as the steak and eggs at Sally's, and Ranger made a fine feast of the heart, which was a treat I couldn't deny him, as he'd stuck by my side for four hundred miles of hard travel, feeding himself, and nary a complaint.

My hand was badly swollen, but I didn't think broken, and I took solace in the fact Mr. Shank what's-his-face was hurting from a dozen spots, and I'm sure nursing broke ribs, which normally put one to moaning and praying for a pain-free breath for at least a month.

I've meet many of his craven kind, and although he came across as hard as horseshoes, I'd guess him a back-shooting coward and would have to watch my rear. Like as not he wouldn't soil his reputation by letting anyone see him do a cowardly act, but he'd fire on me in a heartbeat, front or back, should he have the advantage of darkness and not being seen… or was the only one to be able to relate the story of how I came to be shot.

Deciding the animals and I could all use a day of quietude, I took advantage of the new abode. With the larder full and the horse and mule hobbled in the canyon bottom, happy as pigs in mud, hock-deep in grass and blooming shooting star wildflowers, I settled back, head resting on my rolled up bearskin, in the shade of the tamarisk, to join Mr. Mark Twain on his travels.

As I read, "One frequently only finds out how really beautiful a really beautiful woman is after considerable acquaintance…," I couldn't help but think of how impressed I was with the look of Miss Maddy McGregor, and how I'd once heard that beauty was oft times only skin deep. Too bad I would have little chance to get to know her better, to either prove or disprove the supposition.

One thing I discovered early on in reading the book was that I was sure I'd never enjoy a steamship, as not only the fare was expensive, but it was antici-pated that one would spend as much as five dollars a day for off vessel travel and incidentals. Mr. Twain must have been a man of some means before he ventured forth to Egypt.

Sunday dawned with the smell of dove weed in

the clear morning air, and it wasn't long before I had a frying pan of venison chops crackling while I busied myself with ablutions, including the combing of my hair as best I could. I guessed I looked respectable enough with only two days' growth of beard. I'd used some of the doe's tallow to darken up my leather goods and had combed Dusty to a sheen.

It took some convincing to get Ranger to stay with the mule and guard the camp, but I finally lowered the doe's hide from where I'd hung it high up a tamarisk, as wrapper for meat and such, and pulled out a nice thigh bone from the doe, and the convincing became easier.

Mr. Wong Lee was pleased to see the shiny dime and to loan me his tent to change, and even supplied a mirror, a dash of water, and a fine turtle shell comb to touch up my hair.

By the time the church bell went to ringing, I was as polished as a rough hand with limited wardrobe fresh out of the wild could be, and joined the throng gathering at the steeple.

Miss Maddy McGregor stood with her father at the door, greeting those attending and seemed rather surprised when I appeared and gave her a tip of the hat, a polite nod, and extended a hand to her father. And I was surprised she recognized me, as I don't think that other than when she berated me, she'd ever lifted eyes to mine.

This time her gown was robin's egg blue and her father was dressed in a fancy black frock coat and a store-bought white shirt with a black silk stock pinned with a gold cross that must have gone two ounces if a pennyweight. He was either the best paid preacher I ever saw, or the heir to an eastern fortune...I guessed the latter.

I was barely seated as far against the outside aisle as I could get, when in walked Colonel Mace Dillon himself, followed by a half-dozen of his riders, hats in hand, hair slicked down, all spit and polish as drovers go. I watched carefully for another familiar face, but Shank Cavanaugh had been left to his own devices, and I presume those devices were currently healing up and trying to get over looking like a piece of pounded flank meat.

I was impressed with the facility, which must have seated a hundred, if only on backless benches. And with the upright piano, where Miss Maddy seated herself and began to play quietly, a piece I recognized—you'd have to be a dog-eating heathen not to know 'Tis So Sweet To Trust In Jesus—until her father positioned himself behind the pulpit and lifted his hands for silence.

After a short prayer, a dose of piano from Miss Maddy and some wailing from the congregation, a smattering of whom even sang in key, he launched into the sins of those of us who had come to pay, cash and penance, for the privilege of having our characters besmirched. I almost made it through the whole service before I was called on the carpet, by newfound reputation if not by name, due to the fact that two men had been called to climb the golden stairs only two days prior, and one, currently incarcerated, would surely follow.

He did make mention that the good of the whole evil incident was the fact the town's money was still intact, and that, of course, was the last thing said before the offering was taken.

I ponied up a thin dime, although it pained me greatly to do so.

To my great surprise, as soon as the service was over, the pews were dragged aside with the help of the whole congregation, and tables sat up. Women retreated to wagons outside and as quickly as one might work up an appetite, those same tables were laden with fried chicken and all the trimmings—I was pleased to see I was to get my dime's worth and some to boot. I was handed a cup of some kind of fruit punch, which, to my great dismay, seemed to be missing the miracle of fermentation, but didn't have to pine for long.

Mr. John Pointer soon sidled up beside me and extended a welcoming hand.

"Would you care for a little something to put some teeth in that punch?" he asked.

"Can't say as I'd object," I said.

He looked around making sure he spotted the preacher, who was being admired by a pair of gray headed ladies with girth to match their ages, and looked to be deeply involved in their adulation, before Pointer slipped a flask from his inside coat pocket and quickly topped my cup off.

"Obliged," I said.

Miss Maddy wandered by, not meeting my gaze, until I offered, "That was a well done Brahms lullaby you were playing while we awaited your father."

"Thank you," she mumbled, and looked slightly surprised, probably that I had any appreciation of music that might be played on anything other than a Jew's harp.

The fact was my sainted mother did not neglect my musical education and taught me a fair fiddle, which I seldom used of late.

She glanced back over her shoulder as she moved away, looking a little confused.

"Now, to business," John Pointer said, and got my full attention.

I was hoping the business involved the reward he'd mentioned.

"Mr. Slade, in the short time you've been in Nemesis, you've made it quite clear you can handle yourself in the face of adversity. I know you are on your way to California, but rather than that quite so quickly, how would you like the job of town marshal?"

I was a bit dumbfounded. I'd come to this town to perform what would probably be the biggest crime of murder and mayhem ever undertaken on any of the many rough and tumble towns along the Transcontinental; the slaying, any way I could affect it, of six men, and here I was being offered the job of the town's chief law enforcement officer. It was all I could do not to break out laughing, but that being impolite, I rather asked the obvious, "I presume this is a paid position?"

"Of course. We can talk remuneration in a moment. You do, I presume from your background, know a great deal about law enforcement?"

I presume he was still under the impression I was that "lawman" from Texas, and I didn't dissuade him, but again answered without lying. "Sir, I know only a little about the law, and nothing about the laws of Nevada and Nemesis, but then the job of a law enforcement officer is to execute and enforce what others know about the law. I would do as I was instructed as to the laws of the land...and of Nemesis."

"Well, sir, then what would you say to three dollars a day and found?"

"That's not equal to my last job as a captain in the Union Army."

"What does a captain make?"

"A touch under four dollars a day."

"I'll get that approved."

"A touch under, or four dollars?"

He laughed again. "Okay, four dollars."

"You mentioned a reward?"

He laughed. "Well, there's damn sure nothing wrong with your memory. I'm authorized to pay you one hundred dollars from the city treasury."

"If I take the job, or is that a stipulation of the paying of the reward?"

"You, sir, earned that reward, job or no job. And you'll also take possession of the horses and weapons you captured from those blackguards. There was enough cash money in their pockets to cover the window at Sally's."

That made me smile, if tightly. I continued, "By 'found' you mean a place to hang my hat, with at least two rooms and a decent indoor sink and pump and a privy not too far from the back door and my choice of the local restaurants, limited as they may be?"

He laughed and slapped a thigh. "That's exactly what we mean. We'll provide you with a pair of fine horses, your choice of weapons, sidearm and long gun, from any of those my store offers, adequate ammunition, a copper badge, and an office which you'll share with the sheriff, but you'll have your own desk…and that's in addition to what you've captured. It's the town's office, but the county pays a few dollars a month so the sheriff will have a place."

"And a contract for a one year minimum with a month's severance should my services be no longer needed at some earlier time?" My old daddy said to never sell yourself short. But then again, don't crowd the trough with the rest of the pigs, and I had multiple reasons to become a Nemesis law officer.

Hell, I'd take the job for a dime a day, if he'd said no to everything else, particularly as the last job of pay I had was with the Union Army, and the paymaster seldom caught up with us and it was slightly more, one hundred fifteen dollars and fifty cents a month. Of course, I wouldn't end up as cannon fodder in this job, although I more than likely would have my hide equally ventilated with lead pills. And there were times, as Captain, when you were at work twenty-four hours a day…but come to think on it, it may be the same with lawman.

"Done," he said.

But I was not quite ready to shake on it. "It has come to my attention that Colonel Dillon seems to be the stud duck around these parts. Is he part and parcel of this offer?"

Pointer looked a little offended, and cleared his throat before he answered. "Dillon runs the Lazy

Snake, the bank, and the Paradise Valley Land and Cattle Company over across the way. He doesn't run the town, we do...by 'we' I mean the city council, with me as the 'stud duck' to coin your terminology. Nemesis is located on part of three hundred twenty acres my wife and I homesteaded a month before Dillon showed up around here, bought up some railroad sections, and started consolidating the Lazy Snake. I sold every town lot for every business you see around here, including trading Dillon a couple of lots for a couple of stray parcels he had separate from his ranch...and he's still got a burr under his saddle as he thinks I beat him in the bargain. He may be the stud duck at the Lazy Snake, but he doesn't own Nemesis, even though he acts as if he does from time to time. He was not consulted on this offer, and there was no reason to do so, as he's chosen not to serve on the council."

"Good enough," I said as I extended my hand. "You've got yourself a lawman, Mr. Pointer." As we shook, I couldn't help but think about how much easier it was going to be to discover exactly what, and who, had executed the dirty deed at the Bar M.

As soon as he dropped my hand, he turned and waved to three other men who had gathered at one of the tables. They headed our way.

"Now, I'd be pleased to introduce you to two of the town council."

Isaac Ironsmith was one of them, as was the town doctor who was somewhere on a call, Phinias Pettibone who ran the livery, and Paul Polkinghorn who was the manager of Sally's but was also among the missing as he was not the church-going sort, so that was the five of my new employers.

At least, I presumed, until they discovered my intent was to fill the town with cold bodies.

## Chapter Eight

DILLON WAS up before the sun, as was usual for the cattleman. Chang always brought him his coffee as he finished his ablutions. It was his habit to shave every morning as he felt a clean face showed off his Van Dyck mustache and beard nicely. He sent Chang to fetch Curly Stewart, who'd gone into town and not returned until after he'd doused the house lights.

Curly was awaiting him in the kitchen, enjoying a cup himself.

"So, did Willard have an answer from the Salt Lake sheriff?"

"He did. Seems no one over that way ever heard of Taggart Slade."

"Means nothing," Dillon said thoughtfully. "The man said he came from that direction. No reason the sheriff should know anything bout him, particularly if he stayed out of trouble."

"What's your interest in him, Colonel?"

"You worry about the cattle, Curly. I'll worry about you, the cattle, and every other damn thing that effects, or may effect, the Lazy Snake."

"Yes, sir, no offense." Curly sucked his coffee down and rose to leave. "Anything special on your mind, Colonel...regarding the ranch, I mean," he added sheepishly.

"Is Cavanaugh up and around?"

"Haven't seen him. He's still out of sorts. You hear about the council offering that fella Slade the job of town marshal?"

"The hell you say. They're damn fools, knowing nothing more about the man other than he is a fair shot. Hell, every man in my brigade could have made that shot with a Sharps."

"Still, he's the new town marshal."

Dillon couldn't help but smile. Shank Cavanaugh was as fast with a gun, and as accurate, as any man he'd ever seen, but he didn't take to an injury of any sort, in fact he babied himself with the slightest bruise or even a runny nose. The man was a former bullwhacker, not the kind you'd think was faint of heart, and had killed many a man since...but always with a sidearm, never in a rough and tumble brawl. Still, he was a man to be reckoned with, dangerous as the snake who'd probably sired him. Dillon wondered, should he have Shank put an end to this new town marshal before he became a pain where a pill couldn't reach, or just ignore the man?

Like he did often, he decided to merely sit back and watch. Hell, the man didn't look so tough to him, even if he had beat Cavanaugh down like a chicken fried steak.

The man would probably head out to California after receiving his first month's wages.

I've always been an early riser, and I was up, packed—leaving some of my weapons and gear hidden in the wind cave—and at the front door of my new office with a brass sky to the east just as the edge of the morning sun licked the horizon, melting the brass to white hot.

The door was open, and I entered, presuming there may, or may not, be a jailer at hand. Sure enough, there was a fella with a copper star on his chest asleep in the sheriff's chair, leaning well back, legs propped up, mouth hanging askew, snoring away.

He didn't stir when I walked in, Ranger at my heels. I guess he couldn't hear over his own window-rattling snore. A black iron pot belly stove hunkered in a far corner, and atop it sat a tin coffee pot. Ranger put his haunches down a few feet from the sleeper and eyed him carefully, seeming to be a little distrustful, as I crossed and found the stove and pot cold to the touch.

"Damn," I said aloud, as I had not slowed enough to brew a pot before packing up and leaving camp.

He stirred, Ranger growled low, and he opened one eye. I guess he thought a timber wolf had snuck up on him as he leapt to his feet, slapping as his holster, not realizing his six gun was at rest on the desk top.

"Whoa, there," I yelled at him. "That's my hound, and he won't take lightly to you puttin' a muzzle in his direction."

He stumbled a half-dozen steps away from Ranger, his back to the wall, his sleep reddened eyes still sweeping the room until they finally lit on the Colt's on the desk. Ranger growled a little more ominously.

"Don't pick it up," I warned, but his brain obviously had yet to kick in, and he dove forward and snatched the firearm up, and, as I expected, Ranger was in the air before he could bring the Colt's to center on the big dog.

One hundred twenty pounds of flying Dog, and deputy, crashed against back against the wall, his gun arm wrist in Ranger's big chompers, and him screaming like he was being et by a bear, which wasn't far from wrong.

Sighing, I only hesitated a second before I charged across the room and got between them, yelling, "Ranger, down. Down, boy. Don't eat him till we know who the hell he is."

Both Ranger and I backed away, but not before I had the man's firearm in hand. The deputy's eyes were the size of saucers as he rubbed a bleeding wrist, and eyed the gun rack behind the sheriff's desk as if he was going to go for a scattergun.

"You're pretty much a hard head, aren't you, deputy?"

At least he turned his attention to me and away from the rack. "Who the hell are you?" he asked.

"I'm the new city marshal, Taggart Slade, and I presume you're a sheriff's deputy as I was told the marshal would be working alone."

"You're Slade. I heard about you."

"I'm Slade. And that's Ranger, and he don't much like guns in hands other than mine."

"Humph," he managed, studying his wrist.

"You're lucky if it's not broken."

"No, the damn mutt is lucky, as I'd kill him for sure was it broke."

"You got a name, deputy?" I asked, not too politely.

"Yeah, I got a name. Shorty Snodgrass, from Moline, Alabama, by way of the Confederate Army, if it's any of your beeswax."

I smiled, if a little tightly, then advised him, "Well, Shorty Snodgrass, killing my mutt might take some doin' as you'd have to go through me.  He and I are pretty tight."

"Humph," he again managed, then snapped, "I got to go see the sawbones and he'll be charging me at least a quarter, and more if'n I need some cat gut. You gonna pay?"

"Ain't my wrist, and I didn't swing on Ranger. But I'll take it up with him…maybe he's got a quarter hid out somewhere."

"Very damn funny," he said, and headed for the door, slamming it hard enough that dust motes floated down from the ceiling.

"You're a grumpy old fool," I said to Ranger as I crossed the room to try and find some coffee makin's in a whitewashed cabinet that sat far enough from the pot belly so as not to catch fire. He yawned, chased his tail a couple of circles, then flopped down and put his head on his paws, looking as if he wanted to spit the bad taste out of his mouth if dogs could only spit, while I fingered some kindling out of a box next to the pot belly.

"Señor, the coffee is in the bottom drawer of the *gordo* sheriff's desk."

I walked to the open door to the jail section, and saw the same boy I'd seen before, a little less swollen, with his face pressed to the bars.

"I'm not sure it's fat he's carryin'," I said, "He's thick as Adam's off ox, but looks pretty hard to me."

"Please, *por favor*, do not tell him I said *gordo*."

"No problem. What's your name, son?"

"Angel."

"And why are you in the hoosegow?"

"I am in the *jusgado* because—"

"How about you two shuttin' the hell up," the voice came from the darkness in the other cell.

"Angel and I was about to have a cup of coffee," I said, then added, "And if you want one, you'll show a little more respect."

His "humph" was as loud as the deputy's, but he did quiet down.

"So?" I asked the boy.

"I wanted to know who murdered *mi padre*. And all the gringos in the saloon took offense…maybe because I asked with my Remington in hand."

"Did you aim it at anyone, or fire off a round?"

"No, sir, but I would have if I thought it would help."

"So, you didn't shoot nobody, just asked?"

"I merely inquired," he shrugged, "but they did not appreciate my manner, or so the sheriff has informed me."

"You wouldn't happen to be named for your father, would you, and your last name wouldn't be Sanchez?"

"Si, Señor, all that is true."

"I'll make us some coffee."

"The pump is behind the jail, just outside the back door."

By the time I had the coffee brewed and had poured cups for the two prisoners and myself, Sheriff Tobias Wentworth strolled in.

"I heard you was made marshal," he said, without bothering with good morning or go to hell. He did give me enough of a smile to show off his missing tooth...then, again, maybe it was a grimace.

"I heard that too," I said, blowing on my coffee.

"Is that coffee I see my prisoners drinking?"

"Sure is."

"They only get one meal a day, and that's supper."

"Is this a city jail, or county?"

"Well, technically it's city, but they're damn sure my prisoners."

"Well, I don't starve nor abuse prisoners in my jail, no matter whose they are. Unless they start the abusing, of course."

I could see him beginning to redden around the collar, but he endeavored to hide his anger. Finally, he asked, "What the hell is that hound doing in my office?"

"Our office. I'll keep him on my half, should he bother you."

"And that won't bother me?"

"Your problem, I guess," I said. I figured I might as well get things square between him and me right off, as I figured he thought he was stud horse around the whole state, much less this shared office. After all, he was Colonel Dillon's man in law, or so I'd come to believe.

He stood and merely stared at me, as if I was something he'd cleaned off his boot sole after stomping through the corral.

Finally, he fetched a cup out of the top drawer of his desk, walked to the pot belly and poured it full, then eyeballed me over its rim as he blew it.

"Do you want me to put a chalk line on the floor?" I asked, somewhat bemused.

"Won't be necessary. I'll just give him a kick should he get in my way."

"As you wish...you'd probably do fine goin' through life with a peg leg."

Again he stared at me. "Damn if I don't find you a braggadocios sort, even when it comes to your cur."

"No brag, just fact. Ol' dog don't take to bein' kicked, nor do I, to him being kicked, nor do I to myself being on the toe end of a boot."

"We'll see," he said, and headed for the door, then turned back when he had the knob in hand. "I'm gonna catch some breakfast. You seen my man Shorty?"

"Didn't catch his name," I lied, "but there was a fella here about shoulder high to me and round as you snoozing like Methuselah, when I came onboard."

"So, where'd he go?"

"Said he was headed for the sawbones."

Again, the glare, then he asked, "What the hell for?"

"He was thinkin' of givin' ol' Ranger there a kick. Turned out to be a serious mistake."

The glare was hard enough to pierce the rock walls of the jail, but he didn't bother to press it and merely slammed the door behind his broad butt.

Again, dust motes filled the air. Should I anger the county law enough, at least the rafters would get a cleaning. I had to chuckle a mite as I plopped down in my new chair, behind my new desk, and it seemed Angel had heard the whole thing.

"Señor Marshal, he won't take being talked down to."

I arose from my new desk, grabbed a key ring, walked in and opened his cell and waved him out into my office, shutting the door to the cells as he passed through. I motioned him to a ladder back chair beside my desk, and he took it, looking a little surprised.

"Am I free?" he asked.

"No, not yet, but I want to have a little palaver

with you, and I don't want that other fella to hear what I got to say, you understand?"

"*Si*, Señor. My mouth is sealed."

"Good."

We had a long talk, until I began to worry about Wentworth returning, then I returned Angel to his cell.

The most interesting thing I learned was that Angel and his brother, Ignacio were in possession of a journal which should be of great interest to me.

## Chapter Nine

I DIDN'T WAIT for the sheriff or his deputy to return, rather I placed a note on the door explaining that I was at Sally's and would return shortly.

Wentworth had finished his breakfast but was still sipping his coffee, while he regaled the skinny waitress with stories of his exploits as a lawman.

I joined him at his table, without being invited. He did not jump with joy, particularly as Ranger moved to a nearby wall and flopped down so he could see the whole place.

"How about cackle berries and crisp bacon?" I asked the girl.

"And put my breakfast on the new marshal's bill," Wentworth said.

I eyed him carefully, checking out his prodigious girth. "He only has one breakfast at a time, I hope?"

"Only one," the girl answered, as if he occasionally had two or three.

"Humph," he said, reddening, and still not smiling.

"Sheriff job don't pay much?" I asked.

"Probably a damn sight more than marshal," he mumbled.

"So, I know what the old boy is doing behind bars, how about the kid?"

"He's my prisoner," Wentworth said, a little defensively.

"So, what'd he do?" I had already heard it all from the boy, but wanted Wentworth's version.

"Assault with a deadly weapon, disturbing the peace, resisting arrest—"

"Damn sure looks like he resisted arrest, beat to hell as he is. How many of you did it take to bloody the kid up like that?"

"He's been a rebellious prisoner," Wentworth snapped. "And it never takes more'n just me. That kid is going to prison."

"What's he, about sixteen?"

"He's seventeen, and that's old enough to pay for what you done."

I noticed him looking over my shoulder and heard quiet footfalls, so I turned. The woman was a beauty, even with tiny lines at the corner of her large opalescent blue eyes and rouged mouth. Just enough freckles showed through her paint to be charming and youthful.

Pretty as she was, she didn't look too pleased as she spoke. "He's just a kid, and didn't do a damn thing and you know it, Tobias. He was angry about Shank shooting his poor old daddy down like a dog, but he never even cocked that Remington."

I got to my feet and shed the hat, as any gentleman would, even though she dressed a little like a soiled dove in a lace trimmed velvet gown showing a hint of cleavage between generous womanhood, and looked as if she might have had a past.

"Lizzy Perlmutter," she said, extending her hand like a man would.

I shook with her soft, slender hand as I introduced myself, almost saying my real name as I was a bit mesmerized by those eyes and the soft auburn hair that fell to the middle of her back...not to speak of the cleavage which was hard to keep eyes from.

"So, you're the new town marshal?"

"Humph," Wentworth grunted, but I ignored him.

"Yes, ma'am. At your service."

"Well, welcome. Don't believe everything Tobias tells you, he's a regular blue norther when it comes to telling windy tales."

Again, he humphed, and I couldn't help but smile, nor like Miss Lizzy Perlmutter.

"Are you employed here, Miss Perlmutter?" I asked, still standing.

"Sit down. I'll join you if you don't mind."

"A pleasure," I said and she took a seat between us.

"Actually, I own the place, and appreciate your dropping in. I appreciate the business, and the rest of the customers seeing the law here now and again."

"So, Sally?" I asked.

"Sally went to meet her maker. Consumption got her a couple of years ago. Sold me the place cheap and on time. I send her old mama a draft every month for another year or so."

Swan Neck arrived with my breakfast, with some thick slices of brown bread lathered with butter, and a fist-sized vat of honey to boot. And I dug in, listening to Miss Lizzy trade barbs with the Blue Norther while I ate. She didn't give an inch, and he seemed real irritated that she didn't fawn over him, particularly since I watched and listened.

After they'd slowed insulting each other, the girl arrived again with the coffee, then left, and I asked Miss Lizzy, "What's that girl's name? This is the second time she's served me."

"Bridgid," Miss Lizzy said. "Bridgid Fimple. Been here longer than I have, straight from Cork County, via Boston. She was a friend of Sally's, from the old country." She laughed, and I liked it, then she continued. "She's got lots of butterflies in her belfry, but she's an honest soul and always on time. Of course she rooms here, so it's hard to be late." Again she laughed.

I had shoveled in my breakfast and now my coffee was again too hot to drink, so I waved the girl back. "I am happy to stand Sheriff Wentworth to breakfast, this time," I said, cutting my eyes to him so he'd know it wouldn't be a habit, "so what do I owe?"

Miss Lizzy extended a palm out, stopping her, then turned to me, "You sign the tab here if you're a suspicious sort, if not I just tally it up and turn it into the town council every month."

"Suit's me you keeping track, however I don't put other folks on the town expenses, not in my contract, so I still owe you for Wentworth."

"My pleasure, on the house...Like I said, I like having the law around." She laughed and added. "Still, he owes you for the favor...as it's you I'm doing it for."

I dug in my pocket and dropped a dime on the table for Bridgid. "I'll do my own tippin'" I said, replaced my hat. "Nice meeting you, Miss Lizzy," I said, and shoved my way through the batwings.

Behind me I could hear Wentworth. "Damn peckerhead."

And Miss Lizzy's reply, "Damn good lookin'," she said.

I couldn't help but smile as I've often thought of myself as many things, but good lookin' has never been one of them. Maybe those opalescent eyes don't see so good.

After Slade left, Lizzy got up to leave but Wentworth waved her back to her chair.

"So, you hadn't met this Slade fella before?" the Sheriff asked.

"No. First time I ever laid eyes on him. I was out back when the bank was being robbed."

"So, maybe you'll feel him out...find out his background and such?" Wentworth asked with a bit of a sly grin.

"You can do your own detective work, Tobias," she said, with enough of a smile as so not to be insulting, but you could see she was a bit peeved.

"You owe me, Lizzy."

"How's that, Tobias? I don't remember you doing a damn thing to indebt me."

"I help keep this place peaceful."

"I guess that's true, and I feed you full of whiskey with no pay about half the time, and don't tell Martha that you're sniffin' after my girls. That should make us about even."

Tobias got red in the face and stood so quickly he knocked the chair down to the floor behind himself. Then he leaned forward with his knuckles on the table. "Don't you be using my wife's name in this place, Perlmutter, and don't you threaten me."

"That was no threat, Tobias...." She left the rest unsaid, as he knew she meant it was a promise.

"You're likely to have a fire here some early morning, Lizzy. That would be a shame, this canvas roof and all."

She arose and spoke over her shoulder as she headed for the back of the saloon. "Hope you enjoyed your breakfast, sheriff."

He sputtered a moment, then spun on his heel and stomped out.


No sooner had I plopped down at my desk, than the door swung open and the town mayor, owner of the general store, John Pointer, ambled in. I almost stood at attention, as he looked so much like our departed president, Mr. Lincoln.

"I got a place you can look at," he said.

"Place?"

"Residence. A place the city can rent for you... although it's not in the city."

"How far?"

"Mile or so. Were I marshal, I'd want to be out of town a ways."

"Two rooms with an inside pump?"

"One room, but big as two, and the pump's a short ramble between it and the main house."

"So, who's in the main house?"

"Preacher."

I smiled as I presumed Miss Maddy would be on the property as well, and suddenly an inside pump wasn't nearly so important.

"So, when can I take a look?"

"How about right now. My buggy's waiting."

"Let's see, it's been about twenty years since I went for a buggy ride—"

"Too comfortable to suit you, marshal?"

I smiled. "I believe I'd enjoy being squired out for a country ride."

"Then let's get at it. Wife is watching the store, and she'll eat half my hard candy I leave her too long."

Pointer rattled the traces on the hindquarters of a big bay mare and we headed north out of town, Ranger trotting alongside hardly working up a pant, north along Paradise Road, the only other road leading away from town, except for the east-west road that roughly followed the Transcontinental Line. To my surprise, I learned that the room I was about to see was on property owned by no less than Colonel Mace Dillon himself. That galled me a little, until Mayor Pointer explained that Preacher McGregor rented the place for a small fee, and would be subletting the room to me, so I'd have no call to face Dillon and would not be beholding to him for anything. Still, had it not been for Miss Maddy....

As Pointer reined the buggy into the yard, I could see Miss Maddy herself hanging clothes on the line. To my disappointment, she did not walk over to greet us, but rather Preacher McGregor strode out of the house as if he had a fat beaver in his trap and was afraid it would get away.

As I admired the woman at the clothes line, I remembered Mr. Twain's words, "One frequently only finds out how really beautiful a really beautiful woman is after considerable acquaintance...," so I tempered my enthusiasm, not that I held high hopes for my acquaintance with the beautiful Christian woman nonetheless.

I climbed down from the buggy, and noticed a foot-long piece of stiff wire on the ground, sticking up where the wheel had run it over. I bent and retrieved it, bent it, and stuffed it in my pocket, having a use for it.

As he approached, Ranger trotted by him, paying him little attention, but rather walked right up to Miss Maddy, and allowed her to give him a scratch on the ears. She paid me absolutely no attention. I was jealous of the damn dog.

"Nice to see you, John," McGregor said, hand out to the two of us. "And you, Mr...What was it?"

"Slade," I said, again having to think a second.

"Mr. Slade...or now I guess its Marshal Slade." He looked as if he was sucking lemons when he said it.

"Yes, sir, that's what it is now."

As Pointer was tying the bay's traces to a hitching rail, McGregor headed out toward the barn fifty paces to the rear of the house, at a brisk pace.

"He always got a fire under him?" I asked Pointer as we set out to follow.

"He's a man driven...by the good Lord I guess," Pointer said.

The room was a lean-to on the side of the barn, a good five paces wide and twenty-five deep, the depth of the barn alongside. Hell, there was room enough for a whole squad of my blue coat boys. Even though there wasn't a pump inside, there was a beautiful woman at the clothes line not a stone's throw away. There I go again, thinking about a future that can't be with a woman who seems to detest me who's got a father who looks as if he's sucking lemons every time he looks at me. I couldn't help but laugh out loud.

"What?" Pointer said, "You don't think this will do?"

"Not enough room—"

"Not enough room. My whole family—"

"Not enough room for me, my horse, my mule,

my mutt, and a herd of longhorns," I said, and laughed again.

"Then you want it?" Pointer asked.

It was sparsely, but adequately, furnished. There was a bed, which was made up with a thick down comforter atop, a small side table with a coal oil lamp atop it—a fine place to finish my Mark Twain volume—a dresser with a small looking glass over it, an armoire facing the bed which would hold ten times the clothing I owned, a couple of benches at the far end flanking the bed, which was well away from the pie safe, kitchen cabinet, and lion-footed oak kitchen table seating four also with a coal oil lamp atop it, with spindle back matching oak chairs. One upholstered piece, a love-seat if my memory served me correctly, slightly worn with a God-awful green wool cover—not that I gave a hoot—separated the room into two areas. And two multi-colored oval hooked rag-rugs, each delineating the two sections of the room, would keep the feet warm on cold mornings.

A fella could raise a family in less.

A steamer trunk sat in front of the love seat, serving as a table of sorts, and would do for even more storage.

I turned to the preacher, who was standing at the doorway.

"How much?" I asked, "Including the

furnishings?"

"Not so fast. Are you a drinking man, marshal?" he asked.

"Not to excess."

"Well, some think any is an excess."

"Some can think what they might. Nor do I chew, nor spit on the floor, nor curse unless called for...and never do I take the Lord's name in vain. And I'm very respectful of women folk and other's privacy."

"Humph," he said. "Well, I'm not taking you to raise. It's merely a business arrangement."

"Good thing, as I'm full grown," I said in return, and got the lemon look again. "How much?"

"Eight dollars a week," he said, but I could see he was reaching for a star.

"I'll give you three, and you'll throw in a stall for my two animals, and give me no trouble about the hound."

"Humph," he said, and spun on his heel and headed away.

Pointer laughed and shook his head. "I should have you running the store," he said, low enough that the preacher couldn't hear. "I do appreciate your watching out for the town's money."

"I don't favor throwing money away, particularly not my employer's. Let's go," I said, and headed out the door behind McGregor.

## Chapter Ten

POINTER FOLLOWED me out and I angled for the buggy. Miss Maddy was still at the line, hanging up a pair of the preacher's fire engine red long johns. Ranger, at her side, looked as if he was none too eager to leave...for which I could not blame him, traitorous damn dog.

McGregor paused at the back door to the house and called out just as we reached the buggy. "How about six a week?"

"I'll go four, including the stalls, and a share of that pasture." Two fine-looking matched grays grazed in a pasture of at least forty acres beyond the barn.

"Blaspheme," he muttered loud enough that we could hear, and I continued to mount up to the buggy seat. I waved Pointer up alongside.

"All right, damn the flies and all you Republicans," he said, seeming mad enough to spit.

I couldn't help but laugh and dismounted and walked his way, and Pointer followed. "I guess a fella's politics should be his own business," I said, but with a smile. He growled, so I continued, "And I guess the good Lord will forgive me for driving a self-serving bargain, and will forgive you for the 'damn' which was, I guess, because I did." I extended my hand, and he took it.

"Yes…pardon my language." He looked a little sheepish for the first time.

Miss Maddy had finally stopped her laundry hanging and was staring at her father as if he'd just made a bargain with the devil for his immortal soul.

Digging in my pocket I pulled out the last of my twenty dollar gold pieces. "Here's twenty. That's five weeks in advance.

Pointer growled. "Now, you're pretty damn free with the town's money."

I could see McGregor's eyes flare with the generous pre-payment, and he half smiled for the first time.

"Come in and we'll seal the bargain with some sweet tea," he said, seeming to calm himself. He turned to the clothesline. "Maddy, will you favor our guests with some tea?"

Now it was Miss Maddy who looked as if she was sucking lemons.

It must run in the family.

To her credit, she gave Ranger another scratch on the ears before heading to the back door.

As we headed for the house, I reassured Pointer. "Town can pay me back by the week, should it need to do so."

"Town can pay you the twenty, forthwith," he said, but looked about half irritated.

"Mr. Pointer, Mr. Slade," Maddy said, in the way of a greeting as she brushed by. This time her dress was simple and soft and hung to her ankles, and, I couldn't help but notice, clung to her womanly figure. She was shapely enough that the bustle I'd seen her wear was unnecessary, but you can't figure fashion, nor the thoughts of women who cling to it. One thing was sure, the soft dress clung nicely to Miss Maddy.

I gave her a nod and a tip of the hat, and said, "I hope you'll call me Tag," but she paid no attention.

That greeting was the last thing she said to either of us, as she disappeared after serving us the tea, and was not seen again.

I was surprised by an office full when I returned, ranger close at my heels. Judge Felix Thorne and another fellow I hadn't met, Tobin Stewart, were introduced by Sheriff Wentworth. His deputy, Shorty Snodgrass, leaned against the wall in a corner, his wrist bandaged, his eyes glaring at me with something other than brotherly love. Ranger curled up beside my desk, never taking his eyes off Snodgrass. All of them had coffee mugs in hand.

The judge was eyeing me carefully from sunken eyes, deeply set in a rather skeletal face, under a top hat which was the same shade of dark brown as was his cravat, waistcoat, and finely cut coat and trousers.

Before I took my chair—the others were seated around Wentworth's desk—I asked the deputy, "How's the wrist doing?"

"Nothing killing a damn dog won't fix," he muttered, and I gave him a look that said what I was thinking, until he cut his eyes away.

"So, marshal," the judge asked, "what do you think of Nemesis?"

"Decent little town," I said.

"You've been a lawman, down in Texas, in lots of other decent little towns?" he asked.

"Who told you that?" I replied, and he looked at me curiously.

"You sons-a-bitches," the man in the cell yelled through the door. "All of you can go to hell."

I walked to the doorway separating the office from the cells, and could see my prisoner now had a sling on his arm. I guess the sawbones had visited the jail while I was gone.

"Shut up, or I'll break the other wing," I growled at him, but was happy for the interruption so I didn't have to answer the judge, then closed the door to keep the noise down.

When I turned back I didn't give the sallow man a chance to continue his questioning. "So, your honor, when do these two go on trial, so we can have a little peace around here?"

"We'll pick a jury tomorrow and the next day, can we get twelve honest folks together, that'll take us to the weekend, then maybe next Monday, or Tuesday...give the town folks time to build a decent gallows."

"Pretty sure we'll need one, are you?" I asked.

"You know who you got in there?" he asked.

"No idea, I do know he's got a mouth on him, but other than that...."

"That's not a Hutchin's as he claims. That's Natchez Pete Pelletier, wanted from here to St. Louis, and some farther, for murder and both train and bank robbery. He's got a birthmark shaped like an eye on his upper left shoulder. No question it's him. There's a fifteen hundred dollar railroad bounty on him. We've got three witnesses to a murder in a bank in Wichita headed this way on the train, and another coming up from Colorado, all the way from Leadville...but I have his declaration by way of the wire, should he not get here in time. Another, an ex-railroad guard, now unemployed due to the fact he's got one arm, thanks to Pelletier and his boys, will be in on the Sunday train. No, we've got Natchez Pete cold as a whore's heart."

"And that reward goes to…?"

"Why, to you and to Wentworth here."

That took the smile off my face. "Wentworth?"

"Sure enough. You and Wentworth."

"And to Wentworth because…?"

"Why, he said he was working with you."

I guffawed. "Sheriff Wentworth was home feedin' his face, or hoeing weeds in the garden," I said, not backing up an iota. "First time he saw…what did you say his name was?"

"Natchez Pete Pelletier."

"First time Wentworth saw Pelletier was right there in that cell."

"The hell with that," Wentworth yelled, spittle flying. "We share the law enforcement, hereabouts," he snapped, lurching to his feet, his arms thrown back as if he was about to charge across the room. Snodgrass, like a yap dog, was close at his heels.

I arose slowly, and spoke softly. "You can have half the work around here, Wentworth," I said, "when you're around to do it. You don't get half the money unless you've done something to earn it."

"We'll settle this later," Thorn said, and rose, picking up a walking stick with a knotted silver handle that had been resting on the floor beside his chair. It would serve as a fine weapon, as it was Irish shillelagh-sized, even if it didn't conceal a sword blade, which I suspected.

Wentworth and I continued to glare at each other as the judge headed for the door. He paused as he was leaving, turning back to me. "I'd be obliged if you'd join me for supper, marshal. We should get to know each other as we'll be working hand in hand on some things."

"My pleasure, judge. And my treat. What time, where?"

"Sally's is fine, say at six? And we'll flip for the bill, if you're a gambling man?"

"My pleasure," I said.

Wentworth, with Snodgrass close on his heels, stomped out brushing by the judge.

"You got him a mite angry," Thorne said, a sort of sly smile on his sallow face.

"Not the first time, and I'm sure it won't be the last," I said, not returning the smile.

"He's a decent friend," Thorne said, "and a formidable enemy. Don't push him too hard. I'd hate to have to sit in judgment of one lawman shooting down another."

"I don't push at all, judge," I said, this time the sly smile was mine, "I just push back when need be."

"Humm," he said, thoughtfully. "See you at supper, marshal."

Tobias Wentworth, Shorty Snodgrass still close on his heels, strode away from the office, huffing like the Transcontinental, which was moaning its approach to town from the distance.

"Damn, that Slade is an irritating sort," he snapped.

"You gonna let him have that reward, boss?" Shorty asked.

"I'll get elected president first. Nope, he's reaching beyond the length of his grasp on that one."

"He's a son-of-a-bitch all right. He got himself off to a bad start with the both of us."

"And he'll get the short end of the stick, I promise you that."

"How about I slip that Pelletier a weapon, maybe a blade to stick him with through the bars. I can promise him we'll let him out, should he stick Slade, then claim he was a liar if'n he says I did."

Wentworth stopped short and turned to his deputy. "Shorty, I'll do the thinking around here. That Frenchman would as soon stick you as Slade. Just do your work, let me do the thinking."

"Yes, sir," Shorty said, shrugging.

As soon as the office was empty, I took a key back and let Angel join me in the front, pouring him a cup of coffee—thick enough to float a spoon—that was still warm on the stove.

He sat across from me, pulling a chair away from Wentworth's desk.

"You're leaving here tonight," I said.

"You mean I am free?  I thought they said a jury…"

"They did," I said, "but they'll railroad you right into the penitentiary, and I won't have it. You're out of here in the dead of night.  My mule, Jackson, will be bridled and outside the back door.  You got a place to go?"

"I do.  I will go first to Señor Henderson's to tell my little brother, Ignacio, where I will be in the mountains.  There's a line shack…"

"I want that journal you have."

"I will take it with me, and keep it safe.  Iggy will know where I am.  He will be taking a flock to the meadows around the shack in a week or less, if things are as normal."

"Don't tarry, Angel, once you set out of here. Your Remington is on the rack over there and I'll have a box of shells on the shelf."

"*Sí*, Señor."

"Angel, no matter what happens, don't use that

rifle against anyone who's after you. You'll hang, you shoot someone down while you're on the run, and I don't want to live with you shooting someone, or you getting shot. You understand?"

"*Si*, Señor. The mule, she is fast?"

"He is fast, and steady. You keep at it and you'll be twenty miles or more away come first light."

"And that is as far as the Henderson place. Then I will go straight into the hills."

"Okay, I'll see you in a week or less, probably day after tomorrow, Saturday or Sunday, and I'll bring you some supplies. I've got to be back here Monday or Tuesday, depending upon when old Natchez Pete Pelletier is scheduled to be tried. What direction is the Henderson place?"

"Due west, fifteen miles to the next big trestle which is a quarter mile long, then five miles or a little more south, up the draw that is Dead Miner Creek near the place called Piute Spring. It is hard to miss."

"Fine, tell Pelletier that you want to go back to Mexico, and if you get out that you'll head east to the road out of Salt Lake City, just to throw any trackers off."

"East, to the road south out of Salt Lake City."

"Make sure Pelletier knows." I handed him the piece of wire I'd picked up at McGregor's, and had shaped like a key, and handed him a key to the cell.

"Leave the wire in the keyhole, bent just like I've got it, as if you'd used it to pick the lock. Return the key to my desk drawer. I'll make sure Snodgrass is out of here after I have supper with the judge. When you hear us leave, wait until you count to five hundred...you can count?" He nodded, and I continued. "Then you hightail it out of here, out the back. The saddled mule, outside the back door. Try not to wake Pelletier."

I repeated the instructions, until I was sure he had them down, then returned him to his cell, key and wire in his pocket. Luckily, Pelletier was snoring away, oblivious to all else.

Jackson was at Pettibone's Livery stable and I headed there, paid his bill of fare, and explained to the stout little stable master that I was taking the mule out to my new facilities at the McGregor's, then grained him well, watered him, and tied him behind the jail with a hackamore on and lead rope keeping him at the ready. Angel was young and tough, and could ride bareback.

The judge was a pleasure to dine with, and although he was a bit of a sycophant when it came to Colonel Dillon, he seemed a decent sort of gentleman. Before he had the chance to grill me, I made it clear that I wasn't particularly fond of talking about my past, that the memory of killing men upset my digestion, and I'd just as soon talk of the future.

That seemed to satisfy him. We sat, and talked, with Ranger curled up beside me, and sipped a decent whiskey until almost half past eight, then he excused himself. I purposefully lost the flip, telling him a white lie about which face was up, and bought his supper with most of what little I had left. With luck, the town would be returning my rent money soon.

As I suspected, Shorty was at the sheriff's desk, already asleep. I slammed the door, and he leapt up and ladled a cold stare over me.

## Chapter Eleven

---

"SHORTY, we're going to have to work together, and I, for one, don't like to have bad feelings. I'd be proud if you'd accompany me over to Sally's and let me buy you a few drinks of good bourbon whiskey."

He eyed me, more than a little suspiciously. "You want to buy me a few drinks?"

"Yeah, I feel bad about your wrist and all. How about it?" I gave him my best gambler's bluffing smile, and he folded.

"Sure. Why not? I could use a nightcap."

"Hell, have you eaten?"

"I had a can of peaches."

"The hell you say. That's not fittin' for a hard working lawman. I'll buy you a beef steak as well."

"Let's go," he said, finally managing a stupid grin.

Shorty was short in stature, and quite a bit shorter in brains.

It was midnight and a half-dozen whiskies before I helped Shorty back to his boss's desk, where he promptly put his feet up and went to snoring, not bothering to check on his prisoners. I did so, and found the one cell door standing open, and Pelletier snoring away.

Before I left I checked to see that the wire was left in the keyhole and my key returned to its place in the drawer. Angel proved himself to be an Angel.

With Ranger at our heels, Dusty took me out to my new abode.

I was up before sunup and surprised when I walked into the barn to saddle up, that Preacher McGregor was feeding a couple of shoats he had in a stall with hog-wire around its lower half at the far end of the barn.

"Mornin'," I said, grabbing my saddle off a rack that had had an empty slot.

"Good morning, marshal. I'd appreciate it if you'd flop your tack over the rail to the stall you use, and I'd appreciate it if you'd use the stall next to the pigs."

I started to say that I'd appreciate it if he'd jam a pitch fork in his butt, but didn't. Nor did I sic Ranger on him, as came to mind. Rather, I nodded.

He finished and waited by the barn door until I had Dusty saddled. I started to mount up, and to my surprise, he asked, "I don't guess you've got any supplies yet. Coffee?"

Thinking he was already setting out to be a borrowing neighbor, I merely shook my head.

"Then how about coming inside and letting me pour you a cup? Fella shouldn't have to leave home without a cup of mud."

I was almost speechless, but managed to nod and to tie Dusty to a stall rail, and then follow him in.

Miss Maddy was at the stove, her bruise considerably better, at least the swelling had receded, and gasped when she looked up to see me enter. She was fully dressed, but her hair was up in a pile on her head, and she ran for a door leading into the living area with what I presumed was a pair of bedrooms beyond.

"Father," she called out as she scattered. "The least you could do..."

The preacher laughed. "Women, vanity is a heavy cross they must bear."

I smiled, and took a seat at a beautiful walnut kitchen table, as he poured me a cup and sat it in front of me. "Cream?" he asked.

"No, sir. Never developed the habit. Most of my coffee's been aside a campfire a far piece from a milch cow."

"Cattle droving?" he asked, taking a chair across from me.

"Some, but mostly in the Union blue."

"Here's to the end of slavery," he said, toasting me with his coffee cup.

"And to the country, rejoined."

We drank. I had figured him for a southern man, but now I wondered.

I glanced up to see a fine double barrel shotgun resting on a separated pair of antelope horns over the kitchen door.

"Fine looking weapon," I said.

"Good for coyotes, should they bother my chickens," he said, a bit of a sly smile.

"Two legged ones as well?" I asked, my smile equally sly.

"Only if absolutely necessary."

I was pleased to note he was a practical man, even if a God-fearing one.

"That, sir," I said, "is about as fine a cup of Arbuckle's as I've ever had."

"Compliments to Maddy, not to me."

About that time, she reappeared, a dust cap covering her mound of hair. And if I wasn't mistaken, she'd added a little color to her cheeks and lips.

"As I said, that's a fine cup of coffee, Miss Maddy."

She actually smiled. "An everyday task, marshal. Since you're to be a neighbor, possibly you'd like to join us for Sunday supper? I'll show you some real home cooking."

"I would, ma'am, should the job not interfere. I've found that law enforcement doesn't always respect the Lord's Day."

"Oh, that's too bad. Let me know by Saturday, tomorrow, I guess, and if you can come, the invitation stands."

We made small talk until I finished my coffee, and the preacher walked me out. "I thought you mentioned you had a mule as well?" he asked as I mounted.

I was forced to tell a small lie. "He's still at the livery. I'll bring him, or one of my new horses, out this evening."

"Fine, stall next to the pigs, remember?"

"Yes, sir, next to the pigs."

It was a quiet ride into town along Paradise Road, with not a soul to pass.

Shorty awoke as I entered.

"I guess I owe you a thank you for the steak and too damn many drinks," he said, rubbing his forehead.

"My pleasure, Shorty," I said, and headed for the door to the cells. "You're fine company," I lied.

I slung it open, and feigned a surprised gasp, then turned back. "Where the hell is the boy?"

"What," Shorty said, and ran over to stare at the open cell door.

I walked over and pulled the wire from the keyhole, and heard Pelletier cross to the bars. "What the hell..." he said.

"You didn't see him escape?" I asked the Frenchman.

"Hell no, or I'd have gone with him."

I turned to Shorty, officiously and accusingly, "How the hell did this happen, deputy?"

"I don't... I got to find the sheriff."

"A little late for that," I snapped.

"How about a cup of coffee?" Pelletier asked.

"Sure, when you tell me if the boy said anything."

"I should help my hangman?" he asked with a laugh.

"You should, and I'll throw in some hotcakes from Sally's."

He seemed to think on that a moment, and I could almost see his mouth water.

"And bacon?"

"Yeah, where did he go?" I could see Shorty lean forward, hopefully.

"Last night, after those rotten beans Shorty brought us, we talked a little. He said, should he get out of this hoosegow, he was headed east, to pick up the Salt Lake road south, then all the way to Mexico...A half-dozen flapjacks and I like my bacon crisp."

"I'll get to it," I said, watching as Shorty headed for the door.

Sheriff Wentworth was a little put out when I refused to join the posse he assembled. I told him I was a hunter from the old school, and I'd hunt alone.

"Suit yourself," he said, and mounted up and led a half-dozen men east, none of whom looked as if they'd last the day out. It was all I could do not to smile.

I had another pair of horses that Pointer had promised to me, also stalled at the livery stable, the two that the bandits I'd shot down had bequeathed me, post mortem. I also had a pack saddle there that Jackson had carried all the way from the Salmon River country. I decided to see how one of the horses would pack, and headed that way, then to Pointer's store, where I stocked up for myself, and for Angel.

"God's eyes, marshal," Pointer said, as I stacked the counter full of goods. "You plan on spending a month chasing that kid?"

"Can't be too prepared," I said. "I got to sign for this as you haven't gotten my twenty back to me yet."

He shook his head. "I'll front you the twenty, then take what you owe for the supplies out of it and give you the change when the council approves the expenditure at the next meeting, and I turn in the total of the supplies for your reimbursement."

"Fine," I said, and headed out with both of us carrying an armload. I packed the panniers on either side of my new steel gray gelding, mounted up, and rode out of town into the hills to the south for a half mile before turning west, following Angel's directions.

Henderson's place was little more than a pair of line shacks, a small barn, and a corral, but it had a fine flowing spring, and Henderson himself was cordial, sitting me down at his table for a cup of coffee, laced with a little shot of rye whiskey.

Ignacio, Angel's brother, was already headed west into the hills, driving a flock of a hundred woolies with the help of two shepherd dogs, or so Henderson informed me. Another two hundred head grazed the hills near Henderson's shacks.

"Fine looking sheep," I said, but he ignored the compliment.

"You know, Ignacio Sanchez was a fine man, and his sons are both good boys."

"What I know of Angel, I'd agree."

"But you're dead set on taking him back to jail?

As I heard it, he was just seeking information on the shooting of his father."

"He'll get a fair trial," I said, lying, for if I had my way he'd never see the inside of a courtroom. He'd stay free.

"Not if that damned Colonel Dillon or that scum, Cavanaugh, has anything to do with it, and if it takes place in Nemesis, you know they'll be in the middle of it."

I finished my coffee, walked out while trying to reassure him. As I sucked up the latigo on Dusty and the steel blue, I continued, "I can offer you my word, Mr. Henderson, Dillon and Cavanaugh will not interfere with a trial in my town."

"Humph," he said, almost insultingly, but I understood his reticence, as he had no reason to believe me, marshal or not.

As I rode away, he called out, "I wish I could wish you good luck in finding Angel."

"I understand." I waved over my shoulder.

"Don't hurt that boy, marshal," he yelled from behind. "Like I said, he's a good lad."

I nodded, waved again, and rode out to the east.

Now, to get my eyes on that journal.


Colonel Mace Dillon sat on his veranda, chatting with Judge Felix Thorne. Shank Cavanaugh and Tobin "Curly" Stewart leaned against the porch rail.

"Kind of you to call on me, Judge," Dillon said.

"You know I always do, when in the neighborhood, Mace."

"So, you picking a jury for the Pelletier trial?"

"Yes, we drew lots this morning. Curly there is on the panel...I presume you can spare him for a couple of days?"

"Of course. Civic duty and all that. And the boy, Sanchez?"

"You didn't hear, then I guess you wouldn't have. He escaped last night sometime. Wentworth and six men rode out after him this morning." He laughed. "Seems he stole the marshal's mule."

"The hell you say," Mace said, but didn't laugh. "What did Tobias think about catching him?"

"Pelletier gave him up for heading east to Salt Lake then south. Wentworth will have him by the time the day is out. Slade said his mule was half stove up, so it should be no problem."

"And the boy will go to the pen?"

"Oh, I doubt it, Mace. All the kid did was wave that old Remington around. Didn't even cock it, the way I heard it. Thirty more days in the city jail should do."

"That's not right, Felix. He's a mean kid. Had they not beat him down, he would have killed someone."

"Not the way I heard it, Mace."

"Well, the way you heard it is not the right way. You put that kid away, understand?"

The judge eyed him for a moment, the defiance apparent in his gaze, then he smiled, albeit tightly, and added, "It'll go harder on him, with the escape and all, but I doubt if he'll see the pen. However, it's whatever the law dictates, is what I'll do, Colonel." They stared at each other like two bull elk in rut, about to lower their heads, until the judge cleared his throat and continued, "Well, I got to get back to town and back to work." He rose and extended a hand, which Colonel Dillon seemed a little reluctant to take, but finally did.

"I'll see you soon, Colonel," the judge said, heading for his buggy and the long ride back to town.

"You're welcome to stay for supper," Dillon called after him.

"Got work to do," Judge Thorne said, waving over his shoulder.

"Damn rights. Put that boy away, judge!"

Thorne waved over his shoulder, and climbed into his buggy.

The three of them watched as the judge whipped up his team, slapping the traces against horseflesh and cluck, clucking the horses into a trot.

"I always thought those Sanchez boys...and the old man...were good people," Curly said.

"Don't you have work to do?" the Colonel snapped.

"A' course," Curly said, a little sheepishly.

"Then get to it."

Curly disappeared off the porch, heading for the big barn.

"That rile you a mite," Cavanaugh said, his wounds from the beating Slade had given him, still raw and swollen. He tried a grin, but winced.

"A mite, but I'll be a hell of a lot more riled if you don't get rid of that smartass marshal and the Sanchez kid first chance you get. I'm tired to death of them already, and I don't want that kid popping off about anything his old man might have told him."

"No problem," Cavanaugh said.

"Ask those knots on your head, and those ribs you keep rubbing, if it's any problem."

"Like I said, boss, no problem. I was took by surprise…."

"Well, Shank, I don't like surprises, and you'd better not be surprised again, or you'll be looking for a payday somewhere down the road."

Shank Cavanaugh was not used to being talked to that way, and he centered cold amber eyes on the colonel. "Don't threaten me, Colonel."

"You getting soft on me, Shank?"

"I'll take care of that peckerhead marshal, soon as I can breathe deep again."

"We'll see, Shank, we'll see. Maybe the marshal, the boy, and that damned judge if he sees fit not to do my bidding. You don't need ribs to jerk that iron."

"Whoever, Colonel. I don't give a damn who it is, long as I get my paycheck, and a bonus or two for good work accomplished."

"All you got to do, Shank, is actually accomplish something."

Shank grabbed up his hat, fitted it tightly on his head, then spun on his heel and descended the stairs, one hand on his ribs. He stopped at the bottom, and breathed shallowly for a moment before continuing on.

I passed Ignacio Sanchez, his dogs, and his flock of a hundred sheep only four miles from the home place, and paused long enough to dig a couple of pieces of hard candy out of the steel blue's packs and give them to the boy. He was suspicious and careful, but respectful. Ranger and the boy's two herd dogs did some growling and sniffing, then finally settled into a tenuous friendship.

Three miles beyond, the line shack hunkered in a mile-long meadow, now green with spring grass with a trickle of water down its middle, ending in a pond over an acre in size. Lupine and a few poppies bloomed in spots among the meadow grass and cedars lay thick on the hillsides surrounding.

I reined up in front of the shack which was flanked by the only pair of cedars in the meadow, and dismounted, calling out. "Angel."

No one answered. So I yelled even louder.

A hundred yards away, Angel Sanchez appeared out of the cedars, pausing to carefully eye my back trail.

He trotted over as he'd recognized me, and helped me unload the supplies.

"You got the journal?" I asked.

"*Sí*, Señor." He hustled into the shack and retrieved it.

With some hesitation, I took it from him and walked around the side of the shack and sat. I leaned back against a cedar, opened the small leather bound book, and began to read.

The first thing I found, somewhat a surprise, was another letter from Ignacio Sanchez Senior, addressed to me.

And the first sentence, in his poor handwriting and spelling said, "Señor, by the time you red this, I will probly be *muerta*, murdered."

## Chapter Twelve

---

I TOOK a deep breath with that one. Ignacio was a soothsayer, or at least was well aware what he was up against.

The letter went on with the old man's bad spelling and grammar, which, as bad as it was, was better by far than my Spanish:

When the *caballeros* from the Lazy Snak find out I was alive, and had most likely seen the evil they had done, I know it just a mater of time.

I have decide to test if there was any truth to this Amercan justice that is talked about, so I am gone into town to make sure all the honest citizens of Nemesis know that I am alive, and what I have seen. If I am killed there, at lest there are those who can testfy as to my murder.

So, if this letter reches you, after my death, this is my dying decliration that Shank Cavanaugh, the Lazy Snake riders known as Lamb, I think, and Willy Star, Tat, and the Indian known as Croked Arm, as well as two others I only know by sight, but who ride for the Lazy Snak, rode into the McIntosh ranch, the Bar M, and shot and killed *su hermana*, and her man, and set the fire that killed the *muchachas*. It was murder.

As God is my witnes, I hope they roast in hell and *Diablo* picks his fangs with ther bones, for what they did.

If God is willing, I will live to urnate on their graves. If not, *vaya con Dios*, Señor McBain.

Ignacio Sanchez

So, there are seven, not six. The job has grown. By the time I finished the letter, I could taste the bile in my throat and mouth, and my neck and ears were hot with anger. I took a long moment to remind myself that I had a long row to hoe, a field full of tough oak stumps to uproot, before I was through with this terrible task, and going at it with anger would get me killed or incarcerated long before I had slashed and shot and trapped my way through the lot of them.

Calm deliberation is my friend, I reminded

myself, as I watched a redtail hawk circle above, his eyes filtering every movement on the meadow below. I must be as patient.

I sat and listened to the meadowlarks, the occasional screech of the hawk, and the chatter of a covey of Gambel's quail with their short-long-short distinctive cry while admiring the distant cedar-covered hills, until my breathing was even and I'd calmed myself. Then I went to talk with Angel Sanchez.

Finding him at the rough plank table in the cabin, I joined him, after first pouring myself a cup of black-as-tar coffee from atop his little pot-bellied stove.

"So, did your father discuss this killing at his old place of employment...the Bar M?" I asked.

"*Sí*, Señor. It was a terrible thing, and he was afraid that he would be killed for seeing what he saw, and who he saw."

"And he was, you believe? ...Murdered, I mean."

"He would not let me accompany him to town, when he finally decided to ride in. Riders from the Lazy Snake had been to Señor Henderson's ranch three times, looking for my father, but Señor Henderson put them on a false trail, telling them my father had returned to Mexico."

"Why didn't he?"

"My father was an honorable man, and he cared

for the two McIntosh girls as if they were his own." The boy smiled sadly. "He always wished he had a girl or two of his own, *mi madre* died giving birth to Iggy."

"I'm going back to sit in the shade of the tree and read the journal. I thank you, Angel."

"For what, Señor? I have done nothing."

"You went to avenge your father, and that is something. Family, I have come to believe, is about all we have out here. I kept myself in the high lonely too long. I'm going to tell you something that you must swear to keep to yourself."

He shrugged, and I repeated myself. "You must swear."

"*Si*, I swear."

"On your father's grave."

"*Si*, I swear."

"I am Mrs. McIntosh's brother. The uncle to the girls your father was so fond of."

"You are a McIntosh?"

"Her married name. I'm a McBain, as she was."

"Not Stark?"

"McBain, but that's the last time you'll think on the name, at least until my job is finished."

"Your job?"

"I plan to avenge my sister and her family. I don't trust the law hereabouts, so I will be judge and jury."

"And hangman?" he asked, with some encouragement.

"Yes, and executioner."

"Then we are on the same path."

"No, Angel. You're young. I'm pretty near used up, in miles if not in years. You have a lot to live for—"

"I live for my family, now only my brother, and I will avenge *mi padre*, it is the path I have chosen."

I looked at him for a long moment, seeing the dedication in his continence. He meant what he said, but he was only a boy. "You are but seventeen, Angel."

He smiled tightly. "I know my age, Señor. I kill rabbits on the run, and birds in flight. I can fade into the brush as well as any Shoshone or Piute. And I will do this job, for my sainted *madre*, and my murdered *padre*. I will help you, or I will do it alone."

"You did a fine job escaping jail. You did just as I instructed. So, then, you can help me, but you must take my orders, so we work together, and get the job done."

"You were in the war?"

"I was a captain, with many soldiers in my command."

"Then I will take your orders…so long as we get the work at hand done."

"I'm going to read the journal now."

"And I will check to see if Iggy nears. He should arrive here before nightfall, if he has had no trouble on the drive."

"Be careful, others search for you. You won't be any help if you're back behind bars…or shot dead."

His old .43 Spanish Remington rolling block was on a rack over the door. He took it, and left at a brisk stride, I presume to climb a nearby rise where he could look into the distance.

I sat under the tallest cedar near the cabin, took a deep breath, and, with some trepidation, began to read my sister's most private thoughts.

And I read quickly, as it was Saturday, and I wanted to get back to town by early evening.

Before I was done with it, and it being over fifty pages, I was glad Angel had business elsewhere, as the tears were lining my dusty cheeks. It seems my sister had nothing but, in her own words, love and admiration for me, and was worried sick that she knew not where I was hanging my hat. And she had plenty of suspicions that she was in for trouble with the Lazy Snake riders. She also was worried that Shank Cavanaugh had an eye for her, as he'd dropped around more than once, but luckily Jake, her husband, had been near at hand every time Shank had come calling. She feared the day he wouldn't be, as Shank had studied her with lascivious eyes.

Right then and there, through the tears, I made up my mind that it would have to be something very special for Shank Cavanaugh, and I was glad I'd already had the chance to shame him in front of his boss and his cohorts.

I finished my reading, and lay my head back for a moment to collect myself, and my thoughts.

Saturday night. I was sure the Lazy Snake boys would be coming in to hoo'ra the town, to play a little poker or faro, and to pleasure the sportin' ladies.

Saturday night and they'd be filling their gullets with cheap whiskey. And I damn sure wanted to be at hand, if for nothing else, to see whom the players were.

It was just after nine on a starless, overcast night when I tied Dusty and the steel gray to the rail in front of the jail, then stuck my head in to see Shorty sawing logs, his mouth hanging open like a fly trap, his feet up on Wentworth's desk. I went on in and turned the lamp up enough to check the loads in my Colt's Army model, to pull my cut down saber out and thread my belt though its scabbard, and slip my .44 two shot belly gun into my boot.

Taking a deep breath, I closed Ranger in the office to stand guard, trusting that Shorty would fear my wrath should he harm him, and headed to Sally's

Salacious Parlor of Fine Food and Folderol. The place was packed, cigar smoke hanging down to head high, smelling of sweaty cowhands and drovers and the perfume of pleasure ladies, spittoons filled to overflowing, just as I suspected it would be on a Saturday night.

Bridgid Fimple was working the tables and Lizzy Perlmutter sat in a high stool at the rear overseeing her domain. Sheriff Wentworth hunkered like an old bear at a poker table with three other men who looked to be cowhands, and even the stud horse of the country, Mace Dillon, looking like a Prussian general with his nicely trimmed Van Dyck, sat at a faro table, where both his ramrod, Tobin "Curly" Stewart, and his attack dog, Shank Cavanaugh, played the card game.

A second card table, near the rear where Lizzy Perlmutter surveyed the action, held three cowhands, a fellow looking like a drummer, and Mayor John Pointer. Even the Chinese laundry man, Wong Lee, sat at the bar, sipping a whiskey—which surprised me as Chinamen normally weren't welcome in other than Celestial gambling houses or opium dens. Maybe two dozen others, including a couple of working girls I hadn't seen before, occupied the rest of the stools and tables.

I stood for a moment at the swinging batwing doors, studying the place over the top. Then I hoisted the Army Colt's, making sure it rode free and easy, and pushed my way inside.

Only a couple of patrons, including Shank Cavanaugh, seemed to take notice. I locked eyes with the snake, and he looked quickly away. He still showed his bruises. With that I surmised this wouldn't be the night I'd have to trade shots with him.

I stopped at the bar and ordered three fingers of rye from Polkinghorn, then purposefully slopped some of it on my shirtfront in order to smell as if I had long been at the bottle, drank the last finger's worth, and ordered another, then moved to the table with the three cowhands, the drummer, and John Pointer, as it held an empty seat and they were playing draw poker. I figured a sixth would be welcome. It was a game at which many lonely nights encamped with other Union soldiers had given me some proficiency.

Feigning drunkenness, I stumbled a little when trying to gain the seat. Pointer eyed me with interest.

"You got the rest of my twenty, so I can sit in?" I asked the mayor, slightly slurring my words.

He cleared his throat. "Well, no, but I'll spot you to a ten if you want to join in. How was the hunt?"

"Long, tiring, butt blistering, unproductive," I

said with a frown. "Good thing I took a bottle of whiskey along," then added, "Who are these gents?"

Pointer went around the table, nodding at each man in turn as he introduced them, and I shook.

"Willy Stark, Tate Jorgensen," Pointer began, "Liam...what's your last name, Liam?"

"Toole."

I laughed again purposefully to be irritating, although I was already seething inside, knowing in my heart of hearts that Liam was mistaken for Lamb by Ignacio, then said, "Like a wagon wrench? That kinda tool."

He didn't smile. "No," and he spelled it out, slowly, a letter at a time, "T O O L E," he said.

The drummer's name was Elias something or other, but I paid him little attention.

I'd hit a bulls eye with the first shot. Three of my sister's killers at the first table at which I plopped down. I turned to the next man, a swarthy, sallow-faced fellow with a wicked scar on his left cheek. "And I suppose you're a knife fighter, so your name would be Blade?" I was seated between Toole and Stark, with Jorgenson across the table, which was not to my liking, but I didn't have much choice as it was the only seat left at the table. The good news was it had my back to the wall.

Scar-face started to rise, but Toole put a hand on his shoulder, pushing him back in the chair. "He's the town marshal," he said, and I wondered how he knew as I was not wearing my copper badge. I guess the word had gone around the Lazy Snake bunkhouse, putting the boys on notice about the man who'd beaten the hell out of their big gun, Cavanaugh.

I did note that Toole sported a cut-away holster for the nickel plated pistol he wore, with the tie down now cast off the hammer, and his leather looked to be greased slick with tallow. He was more than a mere cowhand, but then I figured most of the Lazy Snake riders were likely to be as handy with the gun as were with a reata.

"Maybe," the swarthy, scarred one said through clenched teeth, "but he's a rude polecat."

I laughed, and shook him with him hard enough to crush bone. He didn't give an inch, which also didn't surprise me. "So, you got a name?" I asked, still giving him a stupid grin. "I'm Slade. My friends call me Tag...you can call me Slade." I guffawed again.

"I'm Willy Stark, in case you didn't catch it the first time. You playing or just drop by to be insulting and interrupt the game?"

Pointer passed a ten dollar liberty eagle gold piece my way, and Lizzy, sitting nearby and watching the exchange, quickly dismounted her stool and changed the gold for a pile of silver.

"You all right?" she asked quietly as she did so.

"Fine as frog's hair," I said, and laughed stupidly, then slugged down half the three fingers of rye. "Deal me in," I said, ignoring her as the last thing I wanted was her near what I figured was going to come down, and we played several hands after she retreated to her stool.

Polkinghorn climbed atop the bar and rapped a spoon alongside a bottle, gaining the attention of everyone in the room.

"Miss Lizzy," he said, by way of introduction, and everyone turned to her as she rose.

"I got something a little special for y'all tonight," she announced. "Mr. Andre Renee from New Orleans is on a layover on a trip west, and has agreed to entertain with his banjo for our mutual pleasure. Tips would be accepted."

Everyone applauded, and the fat banjo player mounted atop an upright piano along the rear wall, next to the door to the cribs, sucked down a mug of beer, leaving himself with a white foam mustache, then tuned up and struck a lively tune.

It was my turn to deal, and I took the opportunity of Lizzy's distraction to palm a couple of aces, then slip them under my leg. I dealt a hand, then passed the deck to Toole, on my left, after scar-face, Stark, on my right, won a hand. And in passing the cards, I clumsily brushed a couple of my coins off the table.

Toole's coat hung loosely on his thin frame, and while bent and rummaging around on the floor gathering up the coins I slipped the aces into his coat pocket, at the same time fishing the belly gun out of my boot and into my own coat pocket, which I still wore, even though the place was a little on the warm side.

After a few more hands, when I'd lost five of the ten dollars, and downed the rest of the whiskey, Toole, who was a fair poker player, won a big hand with several dollars in the pot.

"Damned if you're not a lucky son of a gun," Pointer said to Toole, as he raked in the pot.

"Either damned lucky," I said, with a low growl, "or a damned cheat."

Toole stood so quickly he knocked the chair back and over, crashing to the floor, and drew his weapon in a flash. He was fast, as I had a suspicion he would be. The room silenced as all heads turned toward the sound.

"You calling me a cheat?" he snarled. The muzzle of his nickel-plated revolver was dead center on my chest, and the hammer full cocked. I was seconds from being toes up, and leaving my sister unavenged.

## Chapter Thirteen

I PLACED both my hands flat on the table, and stood slowly. "Look friend, I'm a little into my cups." I spread my hands to the side. "And my gun is holstered, and yours is in hand. You shoot me and it'll be murder."

Slowly, I put my hands in the pockets of my coat, and opened it wide. "See, the gun's holstered."

He stared at the cut down saber hanging from my belt, then looked even harder at me.

"Tough shit," he said, but he cut his eyes toward where his boss, Colonel Dillon, had risen, and as he did so, shifted the muzzle of the nickel-plated pistol just enough that it cleared my right side.

The shot from the belly gun in my pocket took him dead center in the chest, and his pistol discharged as he reeled back, but holed the plank wall an inch from my side.

The drummer who was seated across the table between Pointer and Tate Jorgenson bolted for the front door. I spun to face Willy Stark, who looked as if he was considering drawing his weapon. I smiled stupidly at both he and Jorgenson, waggling the barrel of the belly gun, still in my now holed and slightly smoldering coat pocket, having to cut my own eyes away for a split second due to the sound of footfalls. But it was only some wise pilgrims making for the batwing doors.

"One left in this nasty little belly gun," I said, "should either of you care to taste it," and Stark looked as if he might doubt it. And I hoped he would. But Stark, who seemed the most agitated and consequently had most my attention, moved carefully and buttoned his coat, a clear indication that he was not about to defend Toole's honor, as the herringbone wool shielded his weapon from a draw.

Jorgenson gathered up his mug of beer in both hands and kept his eyes off me. He would be no trouble, at least not this day.

Quickly, I scanned the rest of the saloon, looking for where another shooter might be. All looked innocent, quiet, and harmless as church mice, except for Sheriff Wentworth and Colonel Dillon. Both of them were on their feet, snarling, but had not palmed a weapon.

Toole, having dropped the nickel-plated pistol, was flat on his back, no threat, clutching his chest with both hands, his weapon at his side, pink lung blood now oozing between his fingers and trickling from the side of his mouth, while his eyes slowly glazed.

It was dead silent in the place, dust motes floating down from the canvas-covered rafters with the reverberation of the two echoing gun blasts. Even the banjo had stopped its plinking, and I noticed the banjo man slipping out the back.

Still surveying the room, I pulled the belly gun free of my coat pocket, changed it to my left hand, and slipped my Army Colt's out and let it hang in my right. I had no idea how many of those in the room were on the wrong side of my wrath, but I had my suspicions, and if I was to go down from a hail of gunfire from Lazy Snake riders, I would go down spitting lead.

I moved to bend low over Toole and even though I was sure he couldn't hear me, whispered, "That's for the Bar M, you slimy bastard."

No one said a word, until Mace Dillon moved over, with Shank Cavanaugh a step behind, to eye his man, who was blowing lung blood in quiet burbles, yet getting quieter and quieter.

He turned to me. "What started that?"

"He's a card cheat."

"And you know that how?"

"Look in his coat pocket. Honest poker players don't palm cards and pocket them for later. Irritated me a mite."

"A mite," Dillon repeated, then he turned to Cavanaugh, "Do it." The man with amber non-blinking viper eyes bent over his co-conspirator, having to grab his side and sore ribs as he did so, and dug into one side pocket, then the other, finding the two aces, and handing them to Dillon.

"Damned fool," Dillon said, then turned to me. "That was a dirty gambler's trick you did as well, and not exactly on the up and up."

I smiled, and shrugged. "Easy for you to say, Colonel. But who's up, and who's blowing blood on the saloon floor? Up and up don't always live to enjoy breakfast at Sally's."

"Humph," he said, and turned to the three cowhands at the other poker table who'd been playing with Wentworth. "Drag him outta here and over to the digger. Tell him I want a five dollar funeral, not a penny more. If he's got more than that in his pockets, bring it to me. He owes me."

Then he turned back to me. "What did you say to Toole?"

"I said he should practice his card handling."

"I don't think so," Dillon said, his eyes boring into me.

I smiled, shrugged, and reholstered the .44.

Wentworth walked over, glaring at me, his coat pulled back over his holster. "I'll have to take those weapons until after a hearing."

I draped my own coat back over my holster and rested my hand on the .44's butt. "Speaking of hearing, you'll be god-dammed hard of hearing, or worse, you try and take these weapons."

He reddened, looked one way then the other, then at Mace Dillon.

"That's enough for tonight," Dillon said quietly, and Wentworth spun in a huff and headed for the doors, muttering to himself. I'd have shot the fat bastard in his broad ass just to see him squirm, but my feud wasn't with him...at least not yet.

I walked over to Lizzy, who was on her feet but hadn't said a word. And I kept the room in view as I sidled up next to her with hat in hand. Funny how beautiful a woman can look, when you've just come so close to meeting your maker.

"Sorry about that, Miss Lizzy. Didn't mean to interfere with business."

"It's not the first time there's been a disagreement over cards, and won't be the last."

"Probably not. Still and all, let's let the city buy

the house a drink. About three dozen in here, I'd guess."

"Twenty seven, to be exact, now that four hit the door at a run, and you put one in a blood puddle looking glassy eyed up at the ceiling. I'm no longer counting him as a customer…for obvious reasons."

"You do keep an eye on things," I said.

"Better than you know, marshal," she said, giving me a strange look, and I thought then that she'd seen me slip the aces into Toole's pocket, but I couldn't be sure. Either way, she had yet to say anything, and I doubted she would.

I gave her a bit of a sad smile, then turned to the three who were gathering Toole up by the arms and legs. "You three, let Miss Lizzy here check his pockets. He owes for some damage to the wall."

They eyed me like I was a leper, but waited as she stared at me. "I'm not taking the pennies off a dead man's eyes."

"As you wish," I said, and shrugged at the three, who went ahead and hefted Toole and headed for the batwings. I returned to the table and gathered up my remaining five or so dollars. John Pointer had said little since I'd sat, and now remained quiet, and a little white in the face.

"Sorry you had to be near that, John," I said.

"Not as sorry as I am," he said, staring at the hole

in the wall. "That could have been a hole poked in one of us," he said.

"Damn sure could have," I said, "marshaling is a hard life, then you get a hole poked in you," and I headed for the doors and out to my animals. I heard Lizzy call out, "You all got a drink coming on Marshal Slade."

I wanted to get the hell out of there before some of the Lazy Snake boys who'd hauled Toole out got their chore done, got over the shock, and set up in one the alleys outside, waiting for me to pass by in the light of some window.

A few of Sally's patrons followed me out, and I kept an eye on them.

One down, six or so to go. But I figured the rest of the lowlifes wouldn't be as easy to harvest as was this first fool.

Preacher McGregor was in the barn feeding when Ranger and I walked in out of the barnyard, now bathed in yellow from a morning sun just coming over the horizon. Dressed in my Sunday best, which meant my only clean shirt, I saw him before he saw me.

"Reverend McGregor, can I help with that?"

He jumped about a foot in the air, obviously startled. Then collected himself. "Danged if you two don't move silent." He shook his head, then added, "I heard you were chasing that Mexican lad. Guess I should have noticed your stock was back." He eyed the steel gray. "Didn't get your mule back, I see?"

"No sir, not yet. Can you give Miss Maddy a message for me?"

"She's in the kitchen. You can give it to her yourself."

I laughed. "Last time I was this early, I think she took offense at being spied on."

"Then what?"

"Please, tell her if it's not too late, I'd like to join y'all for that Sunday supper she mentioned."

"It's not too late. Will we see you in church?"

"Yes, sir. Wouldn't miss it."

I shoveled out my stall and the other four in the barn, ignoring the shoats as that would have been a half-morning job, then saddled up and rode out. I guess I've worn out my coffee rights. Mayor Pointer will get some business from me today as I need to stock up my own little kitchen cupboard, at least with the basics.

In the near distance, dead-centered in the inter-section of the road leading out to the Reverend's place, and on to the Lazy Snake and the one running along with the rails, a pair of carpenters were hard at work on a platform gallows. I guess Nemesis had no problem having rail passengers see what was up in the little town—maybe it is their way of saying "don't break the law in Nemesis." The judge, or the town council, wasn't wasting any time, and the hammering must have seemed quite a presumption for the prisoner left in my cell.

It was early for Sheriff Wentworth to be at work, but his paint gelding was tied at the rail outside our office. He hadn't loosened the cinch, so I imagined him not staying long, or he's just damn hard on his stock.

He was leaning far back in his chair, hands folded in his lap, giving his deputy, Shorty, hell when Ranger and I entered. They went silent but I didn't bother to greet either of them, presuming that Wentworth was still steaming from the dressing down I gave him in Sally's.

"We're going back out hunting that Mexican kid," he said, without so much as a hello.

I gave him a grunt, but nothing more.

"You coming with us this time?" he asked.

"Nope."

"Nope?" he repeated.

"Yep, nope." I said.

"Why not?"

"Church."

I didn't bother to add that I didn't want to be on the lonely trail only ten feet in front of him, and any Lazy Snake riders he might have along. That would be plum foolish. Ranger had curled up near the stove, head down on his big paws, but his eyes never left the big sheriff.

Wentworth guffawed. "You trying to convince folks you're a bible thumping sort...and the blood hardly dry on Sally's floor?"

"As ye sow, so shall ye reap," I said, then ignored him and pushed my way into the cell area, leaving Ranger to watch my back. "You get anything to eat this morning?" I asked Natchez Pete Pelletier.

"That's my prisoner!" I heard Wentworth shout.

"Yeah, and it's my jail," I shouted back. "You want to starve him, take him somewhere else. And we'll get around to discussing whose prisoner he is."

"No, I ain't et a by-God thing," Pete said.

"Hang tight and I'll bring you something," I said.

"I ain't going anywhere," he said sarcastically, "at least not yet."

I eyed him carefully with that remark, wondering if he was figuring on going somewhere soon, or merely meant he was soon heading for the gallows.

As I passed back through the office, Wentworth snapped, "Hold up a minute," then turned to Shorty. "Get the hell out. I got business with the marshal."

Shorty brushed by me, looking disgusted at being dismissed, slamming the door behind himself.

Wentworth eyed me for a long moment, then cleared his throat. "You ain't making Colonel Dillon very happy."

"Ain't paid to, far as I know."

"He's a powerful man."

"Like all of us, powerful or kitten weak, we're only an ounce of lead away from hell."

"Doubt that. Dillon's a God-fearing man, and a pillar of this community.  He and I had a long talk last night."

"Up late were you?" I said, giving him a lazy grin. "Fella your age should get his sleep."

"I only got about ten years on you, Slade.  I still ain't lost my quick, nor my bull's eye accurate."

Ranger picked a good time for a low growl to rumble his throat.  Wentworth cut his eyes at the dog.

"Bully for you, Wentworth.  So you know, I don't give a damn for Dillon nor his cur dogs.  I'm hungry, so if you got something to say...?

"Dillon and I both say, why don't you resign and get the hell out of Nemesis?  You got a piece of that reward—"

"A piece, hell...I got all that reward coming."

"Either way, you'll have a pocket full of money and can ride out whole and go back to whatever you were doing before you dragged ass into Nemesis."

"That what you and Dillon stayed up late to chew over?"

"That was the most of it."

"Okay, just so you know, I didn't have to stay up late to give you both an answer."

"And that is?"

"Go shit in those ten dollar hats you wear." I tipped my two dollar one, and left him sputtering.

## Chapter Fourteen

SALLY'S WAS empty except for Bridgid Fimple, sitting at the bar sipping a mug that I presumed was coffee, and Paul Polkinghorn behind the bar. She jumped to when I came in and got front and center where I sat, with my back to the wall. I pointed to a corner, and Ranger walked over and flopped down, his big brown eyes surveying the place continually.

"Howdy," she said. "Coffee's brewing. What can I get you, marshal?"

"Beefsteak and three cackle berries, toasted bread if it's fresh, and maybe a slaver of jam...and you can bring Ranger a bone if one's lying about."

"And company," she said.

"How's that?"

"Miss Lizzy said to fetch her should you come in."

"Pretty damn early for the late hours she keeps," I said, as much to myself as to Bridgid.

"She does her books and writes letters in the mornings. I'll run out to her place and tell her you're here."

In moments, Lizzy appeared from the back, carrying a couple of mugs of coffee.

Without being invited, she settled in across from me, after we said our hellos, and sat studying me for a moment before she asked, "You sleep well last night, marshal?"

"I did, and I'm in fine fettle this morning. And you?"

"I did, but then I didn't set someone up to get shot down like a dog."

It was my turn to eye her for a moment as I gathered my thoughts. "Well, Miss Lizzy, he was holding a gun centered right on my gizzard. That's what got him shot."

"That's not what got him accused of being a card cheat."

"So."

"So, you slipped those aces in Toole's pocket. Why?"

That caused me to sigh deeply, and her to continue to eye me as if I had the pox. Finally, I offered, "I got my reasons, Lizzy."

"So, maybe you do, but my reasons for keeping

quiet about it are what?"

"What do you mean?"

She waited to answer as Bridgid reappeared with the big enamel coffee pot in hand and a bone the size of an Irish shillelagh protruding a foot out of her apron pocket. The rail-thin Irish lass topped off what little we'd drunk. Then she walked over, gave Ranger a scratch on the ears, dropped the bone in front of him, then moved back to the bar to fill her cup and Polkinghorn's, then disappeared back down the rear hall.

Lizzy continued, while Ranger crunched the big bone with a crack that rang across the bar. "Tag, you sat a man up to be shot down, then shot him down without hardly a blink. I don't abide by that kind of thing, particularly not in my place of business. Believe it or not, folks tend to stay away from places where they think they might die real easy." She let that sink in a moment, then continued. "Now, I got no feelings about Toole one way or the other, the man was ugly inside and out, a scum suckin' swine to my way of thinkin', but I don't condone any man getting shot down without reason." There was a long silence as we sipped our coffee. When I didn't respond, she asked, "So, did you have a reason, other than just by-God meanness?"

I cleared my throat, and leaned a little closer to her across the table.

"I had a damn good reason, Lizzy, but if I tell you, then I put myself at risk, and probably you too."

"I'll take my chances, and do every night here amongst the goober shells, the blood, and the beer, and most every kind of killin' firearm and blade known to man."

Ranger distracted us both with his bone crunching. Again, I sipped my coffee and wondered if I could trust her. I hardly knew the woman, but then she had kept quiet about me slipping the cards into Toole's pocket. Did she do so just to keep a war from erupting in her place of business...or to keep me from being shot down by a half-dozen Lazy Snake riders?

I sighed deeply. "Do you like how this town's being run?"

"Truthfully, I don't plan to make a long nest here, so I don't much give a damn, so long as they don't get in the way of my business. Won't be long before the bore worms can have every board in Nemesis, for all I'll care."

"Fair enough, but you said you didn't like to see a man shot down for no reason."

"I did."

"How about a man, a woman, and two little girls?"

She was quiet for a long time, until after Bridgid arrived with my breakfast and sat it and utensils in front of me, then topped off our coffee and retreated.

It was Lizzy's turn for a deep sigh, then she asked, "You don't think the fire at the Bar M was just a fire?"

"I know it wasn't."

"How?"

"Ignacio Sanchez was a witness."

"I was afraid of something like that. So, who did it?"

"All you need to know, for your own good, is that Toole was one of them."

"And your interest in the matter?"

"Lizzy, I am a lawman after all."

"Yes, and the judge and executioner, I see. But it's more than that."

I smiled tightly at her, and she repeated herself, slowly and with more emphasis.

"Tag, it's more than just that."

Again I sighed deeply before answering, and finally said, "Sarah McIntosh was my sister."

"Oh, sweet Jesus." She sat for a long time as I devoured my steak and eggs, eyeing her on occasion over a fork full. Then she arose and shook her head in consternation. "Try and keep it out of Sally's," she said.

"You're the only one under God's great sky who knows this, Lizzy. And I'm depending upon you to keep it under your bonnet. It could mean my life if the others find out."

"Others...how many are there?"

"It doesn't matter. And you don't need to know."

"Alright, alright, so I don't need to know. But I imagine it'll mean your life, nonetheless, but that's your business, Tag. I'll stay the hell out of it so long as you keep it out of my place of business. You won't tell me who else was in on it?"

"Can't, Lizzy. You'll know soon enough."

"So, I can count the bodies as they stack up?"

"Yep," I said, but with no joy.

She walked away, shaking her head, leaving me to wonder if I'd been a damn fool in telling her. Then again, I had little choice. She disappeared out the back door.

After leaving Bridgid a tip and finishing my coffee, I doffed my hat and walked out, only to find Lizzy waiting in the shadows outside. She sidled up next to me and said, "Walk with me a little."

"My pleasure," I said and we strolled.

"The night we heard about the fire out at your sister's place...it was a Wednesday, as I recall...."

"What about it?" I asked.

"Six Lazy Snake riders came in my place. Unusual, as I normally only see them on Saturday night."

"And?"

"And I could see something was up. They talked real quietly, which was unusual in itself, and drank themselves into a stupor."

"But not a bit of remorse?"

"Not so you'd notice."

"Who were they, Lizzy?"

"I normally wouldn't spread rumors, but they smelled of kerosene and smoke. I wondered at the time...."

"So, who?"

"Toole. Zaragosa. Cavanaugh. Stark. Jorgensen. The Indian, Crooked Arm, was there also, but I don't allow him inside. He was out on the boardwalk. Cavanaugh took him a bottle out there. And Dillon's nephew...but I can't imagine...."

"Dillon's nephew?"

"Seth...Seth Rheinhart, a nice young man. Not like the rest of them."

"But he was there. Ignacio named him."

"He's a nice young man, Tag."

My tone hardened. "He was there, and my sister, her two girls, and her husband, nice as they were, burned just like they were in hell."

"Do me a favor and keep it out of my place," Lizzy said, and started back to Sally's, then stopped and turned to me. "All of this is your business, Tag. I'll say nothing to nobody."

"I appreciate that, Lizzy. I'll save you a seat in

heaven. Or at least recommend you should be sent the other way...which is more than likely."

"You do that, should I change my ways and get a ticket." She smiled sadly and walked away.

I slipped into my office and let Ranger out, then followed, mounted, and reined away toward the McGregor place, and what I was sure would be a good night's rest, as I knew my task.


Tobias Wentworth cancelled his hunt for Angel and had made the long ride out toward the Lazy Snake at a cantor, tiring his horse badly. He found Colonel Dillon, already in his Sunday best, heading into town with a half-dozen riders following.

"What brings you here, Tobias?" the Colonel asked as Tobias spun his horse and reined up beside him.

"Need to talk, Colonel, in private. Figured you'd be riding in."

Dillon waved his men away and they dropped back a few horse lengths.

"What's the problem?" Dillon asked.

"That peckerheaded marshal, that's what."

"He gettin' on your nerves, sheriff?"

"Damned if he isn't."

"Hell, marshals are a dime a dozen here abouts. Why not take him out to hunt down that kid and maybe have your gun misfire...about the middle of his back, I'd think. He's a little hard on Lazy Snake hands, and I want him gone before I have to advertise and fill my bunkhouse with greenhorns."

Wentworth chuckled. "Would be fine, blowing the peckerhead's backbone to splinters, 'cept he won't go outside of the city limits with me in tow."

"Smarter than he looks, is he?" Dillon asked, but didn't await an answer. "I guess if he got shot down right there in town, no one would much give a damn...no one that matters, anyhow."

Wentworth sighed deeply. "To be truthful, Colonel, as much as I dislike the peckerhead, I don't think it's my place to settle your grudges. Judge Thorne would take exception—"

"Thorne doesn't have to know everything that goes on in Nemesis. He's got a lot of territory to cover, and he'll be off riding the circuit soon enough."

"So, how much would it be worth to rid yourself of this Slade?"

"A couple of hundred wouldn't break me."

"You wouldn't notice a couple of thousand. Hell, a couple of hundred is hardly worth the risk. Maybe you should wait until Cavanaugh heals up as he's a real hand at dirty work."

"And maybe I'll just have Cavanaugh open season on all the lawmen who hang their hats in Nemesis?"

"Is that a threat, Colonel?"

"Just do your part, and keep your easy job. Talk Slade into climbing on the train and heading out, and save us all a lot of trouble…not than Shank will like that as he wants to see the marshal squirm with a bellyful of hot lead."

"That I can do, free of charge. I'll have another talk with Slade, and try and send him on his way."

"Don't waste a lot of time doing so, as Shank is healing fast, as you can see. He's with us today and he's been pokin' holes in peach tins for the last two days."

"I'm going on ahead. I ain't et yet."

"Go on into Sally's and have a plate full of eggs and peppers. You need something to heat your blood up, sheriff. You're gettin' a little chicken-hearted."

"Don't count on it, Colonel."

"Talk's cheap, Wentworth. Talk is cheap."

"Humph," the sheriff said, and spurred his horse away from the group.

I returned to my office and was not disappointed that neither Wentworth nor Shorty were anywhere in sight, then remembered I'd promised Natchez Pete some breakfast and had to return to Sally's. In the meantime, John Pointer and the judge, Felix Thorne, had come in to grab a bite to eat.

"Mind if I join you while I wait for a take-out order?" I asked, and they waved me down into a seat.

"A little excitement last night?" the judge asked.

"Just a card cheat, too damn fast to pull his gun," I said. "Could 'a ended peacefully, but he lay down on me and I had no choice."

The judge turned to Pointer, who added, "That's the way it came down. This Toole fella pulled a gun, fast as I've ever seen, and had it full cocked before Slade here could blink."

"So, you got the best of him in the end, it seems?" the judge said, eying me carefully.

"I did, luckily."

"Sometimes stealth is better than speed," he said.

"Usually," I said. "A fella oughta keep his eyes on his business."

"He was Colonel Dillon's man, and Dillon was here?" the judge asked.

"He was," I said, "but he saw it was justified."

"Be careful with Dillon," the judge advised.

"I'm careful with everyone, judge," I said.

"Be extra careful with Dillon," he said.

"He above the law?" I asked, and could see Judge Thorne bristle.

"No one's above the law, marshal. You should know that."

"Well, sir, this is the frontier, and some strange things happen out here."

The judge's words came through clinched teeth. "Not when I'm the judge," he said.

"Hope so," I said, and Pointer cut in, as if he thought things had gone far enough. The mayor was looking a little pained.

"It was cut and dry, judge. Toole drew on Tag here, and he had little choice."

"And," Judge Thorne added, "you'll not be treated any way different than Colonel Dillon would, nor he than you, marshal. Lawman or no lawman, you have to abide by the law, and so does Dillon."

I nodded, knowing than money talks and bullshit walks, and hoping the judge wasn't walking on me with his brand of B.S., and just then Bridgid appeared with a tin plate full of food. I tipped my hat to the two men, possibly leaving them with a little indigestion, and headed back to my office.

"Bring the plate back, please," she called behind me.

I'd just given Natchez Pete his plate when the church bells began to chime.

"Where's the coffee?" Pete called out as I headed for the door. I took a moment to pour him a cup of cold mud from the pot on the pot belly stove, and listened to him complain until I shut the front door behind me.

Dusty was still tied at the rail outside the office. I'd planned to take him to the livery so he could have the run of a stall and a handful of oats, but instead just said, "Sorry boy," and dropped the saddle onto the hitching rail, then headed to church on foot.

Maddy, this time in a blushing pink-bodiced dress with a lace wrap, and her father, in his fancy frock coat and a low-cut top hat, were at the doors, greeting folks. She saw me coming from a hundred-foot distance, whispered something in her father's ear, and disappeared inside. I shook solemnly with the reverend, who glanced down to see I was packing my .44 then back to give me a frown. He started to speak, but was interrupted when a miner to my rear stuck a hand out to pump his. I tipped my hat, removed it, and entered, ahead of the potential chastisement.

The church, to McGregor's credit, seemed to attract settlers, miners, railroad workers, and drovers from near and far, as there were a number of faces I didn't recognize. I did recognize the silence that fell over the place when I entered, taking a seat in the second row from the back, but then the chatter resumed. I guess the word of last night's killing had already made the chatterbox rounds.

Colonel Dillon and his pack were noticeably absent, as the back row where they'd last sat was empty. Apparently everyone knew that was the herd bull's spot.

Maddy and her father walked in from the rear

and we locked eyes for a second from a good distance, but I got no acknowledgement from her as she cut hers quickly away. I was rapidly getting the impression I was, as I think the Latin phrase goes, *persona non grata* again...and there goes my home cooked supper. Obviously, she'd heard of Toole climbing the golden stairway...or more likely falling in a deep dark hole with hell's fire at its bottom.

She played a hymn or two then her father took the podium, led us in a hymn, which I croaked along with until I was distracted by some commotion, and turned to see Dillon and his murder of Lazy Snake crows enter, taking no particular care to be quiet.

Colonel Mace Dillon's Spanish spurs rattled a jingle-bob tune, and he removed his ten dollar hat as he crossed to the bench. This time he wore a red neckerchief, but still sported the diamond stickpin and a fancy store bought shirt that looked like it might be of Chinese silk. A silver-studded belt buckle the size of my palm and carved leather boots with the striped pants tucked therein completed the outfit. He looked peacock proud, and a little barn-yard cock foolish, to my way of thinking. He was not healed, probably having the courtesy to leave his sidearm hanging on his saddle, or in his buggy should he have brought one.

His men, like me, lacked that courteous affectation.

Shank Cavanaugh led the pack following Dillon, and rather than take a seat with the others, moved to my side of the aisle, moved right in behind me, and plopped down. He was the least courteous of all, wearing two side arms, each butt forward—he was loaded for bear. That made my gut knot a little, but I couldn't imagine him drawing on my back in the Lord's house. Rather, his boot began a steady tap on the back of my bench until I turned, and, over my shoulder, spoke to a homely homesteader woman next to him, who had three step-stair kids to her right, shirts made from barley sacks, and Cavanaugh to her left in a black cavalry shirt with pearl buttons.

"Ask your kids to keep their feet off my bench, please," I said to her, ignoring Cavanaugh. He grunted, and she looked very confused, only giving me a nervous smile.

Cavanaugh went from two/four time with the boot to four/four. This time when I turned, I looked him square in the eye. "You feeling your oats there, donkey?"

"You bet," he said, glaring at me.

"Them ribs couldn't have healed in a week."

"Don't need ribs to draw, and my draw is just fine. Tested it just again this morning. Heard how slow you was when you chicken shot ol' Toole."

"You say chicken shot, I say save-my-ass shot, but that's neither here nor there. You're the subject at hand at the moment, so let's step outside. Wouldn't be fittin' to mess up church services."

I rose, as the homesteader woman gathered her kids to her as if she was a hen wrapping chicks in her wings, and half the congregation turned and eyed Cavanaugh and me. I got to the end of the row and waited for him, hands hanging loosely at my sides…as he brushed in front of a half-dozen wide eye staring homesteaders. When he pulled out of the aisle, only three feet from me, I stepped into him and drove a hard left uppercut into his plexus, just short rib height, where I figured he was sporting some splinters, at the same time snatching one of his guns from its holster with my right hand.

He made a croaking sound like a stomped-on bullfrog and crashed to the floor in a heap, going purple in the face. I stooped and gathered the other gun so he'd get no ideas.

"And you thought I'd go outside with you?" I couldn't help but guffaw a little.

"Bastard," I heard the sound ring across the room from the other side of the aisle, and saw Mace Dillon on his feet.

But he held no weapons, and his gaggle of men looked confused.

## Chapter Fifteen

MOST OF THE congregation were suddenly on their feet, and some women who didn't have children at hand to protect retreated to the front of the room, where McGregor had suddenly stopped his spiel. I turned to the mass of now standing folks.

"Mr. Cavanaugh has had a spell of some kind, ladies and gentlemen. I think it best he rest a while in my jail."

A buzz went over the room. I could see the rest of the Lazy Snake boys edge forward, so I jammed the barrel of one of Shank's revolvers deep into his rib cage, and he bellowed the bull frog mating call again. I shook my head at the Lazy Snake boys, a silent warning. Mace Dillon said something I couldn't hear, and they retreated to their benches. But they didn't look a damn bit happy.

Easy as eating a piece of Sally's apple pie, I led Cavanaugh out, speaking low to Dillon as I passed. "You fellas sit tight. I'd hate to have one of you go down just outside the church door. Although it would be handy for the services."

He glared at me, but didn't respond.

It was a long walk to the office and jail, with Cavanaugh gasping and sucking short wind with every step. I enjoyed every pant, wince, and whine coming from the man.

Ranger greeted me with a hard look as if he knew there was trouble at hand, and greeted Cavanaugh with a low growl, but didn't bother rising. I guess he figured Cavanaugh little threat by the pained look still on his face and the fact he was gaspin' like a catfish on a mud bank, and had those ugly amber eyes shut most the time.

With my prodding encouragement Cavanaugh took Angel's cell, across the aisle from Natchez Pete. He was still gasping in pain, only opening his eyes long enough to find the stone bench that served for a bed, as I locked the cell door.

"You're dumb as a slimy tater slug, Cavanaugh," I said, as I headed to the office.

He tried to say something, but his ribs must have hurt him something terrible, as all he got out was another grunt.

Just to be on the safe side, I took down the

double barrel sawed-off that hadn't seen use for some time, I gathered, as it was well covered with dust. I cleaned it quickly with a handkerchief and loaded it with a couple of brass shells I knew to be packed with cut up square nails, pocketed a couple more for good measure, then checked the loads in my .44 and took a seat to see what transpired.

It wasn't long before the door swung aside, me with the scattergun on my desktop, the barrels pointed doorway center and my hand casually on its receiver, hammers cocked.

To my surprise, it wasn't a Lazy Snake rider or Mace Dillon, but rather Judge Felix Thorne.

He saw the double barrel and extended both hands in obvious supplication, and I swung it aside and let the hammers down.

"What are you holding him for?"

"Who?" I said, with a sly smile.

"You know who. Dillon's man."

"Breaking wind in church," I said, and couldn't help but guffaw slightly.

"Don't be a smart ass, Taggart. You got a charge against him?"

"I guess you could say disturbing the peace."

"And the bail is?"

"Twenty-two thousand five hundred dollars and fifty cents."

Thorne sighed deeply. He gave me a disgusted look. Then asked again, "What's the bail?"

"I will release him on your recognizance, judge. You look to be a man of good character."

"No, you won't. You'll release him on Colonel Dillon's good name."

"I don't know how good it is, but if you say so."

"Fetch him," he said.

I didn't move, but merely returned his hard look.

"Fetch him," he repeated.

"I guess they don't teach manners in law school," I said, smiling again, and rising.

"I didn't go to law school. I studied at Wilheim and Roberts in St. Louis. And no, they don't teach manners there, but I'd appreciate it if you'd fetch him so I can get Dillon and his men to ride out of town before there's hell to pay. I'm doing you a favor here, Slade. And should I need to give you a please in order to do you a favor?"

"Don't remember asking for any favors, but I appreciate it none the less."

"Then fetch him, before the street is filled with Lazy Snake riders."

"Yes, sir," I said, and headed for the back, but I closed the door between the office and the cells before I let myself into Cavanaugh's little abode. I crossed the cell in two quick strides, and jammed a boot heel deep into Cavanaugh's ribcage, deciding

I'd convince him to stay out on the ranch for at least a few weeks. He cried out like a chubby-bottomed schoolgirl who'd sat on a cactus, then rolled to the floor, gasping for breath and in pain. I was eyeing him, looking for blood from the mouth, hoping I'd shoved a rib into a lung, but I wasn't so fortunate.

In a heartbeat, the door flung aside, and I palmed the .44, but it was again only Judge Thorne.

"What the hell happened?" he demanded.

"Clumsy fool fell off his bench onto that hard floor," I said, with concern in my voice.

Natchez Pete, who I guess had seen the whole affair, began to laugh out loud.

Thorne turned to him. "That true?"

"Hell if I know," Pete said, between bursts of laughter. "He does look like a clumsy sort," he said, the smile not leaving his face.

Thorne and I both managed to get Cavanaugh to his feet, and Thorne, talking to himself, led him through the office and out to where a pair of Lazy Snake boys waited.

It was the one called Willy, and another, the Mexican, but he was across the road, his wide flat-brimmed hat pulled low. He wore a serape, one of those blankets with a hole centered to put your head through. He mounted up and I never got a good look at him. They had a mount for Cavanaugh, and I got a little chuckle when Willy had to practically lift the gunfighter into the saddle. They rode out, with the Mexican joining up with them. I did note that the Mexican rode a spotted Appaloosa, white on gray, and Willy a sorrel. And the sorrel was missing a right rear shoe.

After watching them ride on, I returned to my office.

"That'll cost you some more hotcakes," Natchez Pete called from his cell, still chuckling.

"Damned if you didn't earn them," I yelled, keeping my eyes on the front door, expecting an invasion of Lazy Snake riders at any moment, but it didn't come.

It was late afternoon when Wentworth and his late starting posse rode back into town, and he didn't bother to come to the office. I guess his wife had another pullet in the frying pan, but Shorty did show up and plopped down in Wentworth's chair.

"Do any good?" I asked, knowing the answer as they'd ridden in from the east again.

"Nope, not a sign. I think that kid is halfway back to Mexico by now."

"Damned if you're not right," I said, agreeing.

"I don't guess you got a bottle in that desk of your'n?"

"Nope, but I'm heading out early as it's Sunday and all, and I'll fetch you up one from Sally's."

"How about some good stuff?"

"I'm buying. How about some rotgut rye?"

"Sounds fine to me."

By the time I rode into the home place it was late afternoon. As I was unsaddling Dusty, McGregor exited the house and walked straight toward me.

"Maddy's not feeling well, so supper is off."

"Not surprised," I said, not bothering to turn.

"Another thing…"

This time I turned to face him, as there was no reticence, but rather seriousness in his voice.

"And that is?" I asked.

"We think…Maddy and I think…"

"Spit it out, reverend."

He seemed to gird himself, then continued, "We think it would be better you found somewhere else to bunk."

"You do now, do you?" I could feel the heat on the back of my neck, so I was extra careful with my words.

He merely nodded.

"Well, sir, I paid for a month in advance, and when that paid for month is up, I'll find another place to bunk."

"I'll return your unused money…"

"Nope, I paid for it, I'm using it up. If I'd 'a wanted the money, I'd 'a kept the money. I need the room for a while longer."

He mumbled something, but turned and started for the house.

I called out to his back, "Tell Miss Maddy I appreciate the supper offer, and am real sorry she's under the weather. I'll take it another time, should she feel better."

He turned and glared at me a moment, then just shook his head disgustedly and disappeared inside.

The pressure of taking Cavanaugh out of a church full of folks under the glare of a half-dozen of his mates was exhausting I guess, as falling into my bunk, even without my supper, was like I'd been poleaxed with a sledge.

But even I couldn't sleep through what sounded like a grizzly bear on the rampage. I leapt out of bed, pulled my trousers and gun belt on, and, without my boots, headed out my door which was standing wide open. A pitch dark, moonless night awaited and I stopped short when the growling was punctuated by a gunshot and the cry of a dog, which could only be Ranger.

Palming the .44 I charged to the left at the sound, wanting to fire at a commotion I could barely make out from the light of an oil lamp from one of McGregor's windows.

But I couldn't fire, as it might be McGregor, then the flash and booming reverberation of another gunshot and an ounce of lead whistling by my ear made up my mind, and I cut loose.

The next yelp was that of a man, and I heard footfalls as he charged away into the night. And I charged after him, then fell on my face into the deep dust of the barnyard. It was a good thing I did, as the crack of a pair of Winchesters roared out of the darkness and bullets cut the air over my head.

The whine behind me was Ranger that I'd tripped over, and who'd probably, if accidentally, saved my bacon again. He was on the ground, whimpering. A jolt of almost incontrollable anger shook my backbone.

Through McGregor's window I could see a man, face covered by a neckerchief, standing in the kitchen, holding a gun on Maddy in a nightgown and her father in a nightshirt. The man was staring lasciviously at her, sweeping his eyes up and down— that, too, shook my backbone.

My anger was such that the door was barely an impediment as I charged into the kitchen. He tried to swing on me, but the .44 crashed across his skull before he had the chance.

He went down in a heap and I swept up his gun, whacked him another stout one across his noggin, and yelled at Maddy, "Douse that damn light!" I holstered my .44, reached up over the kitchen door and gathered up Reverend McGregor's double barrel, then raced back outside, only this time through the living room and the front door on the opposite side of the house, and out into the sagebrush, making a circle around to where I thought the rifle shots had come from.

From farther out in the brush I heard the sounds of at least two men, and cut loose with one barrel of the shotgun, then heard the pounding of hoofs, and fired the other barrel. Some yellow cur yelped like he was scorpion stung, but then another set of hoof beats disappeared into the darkness.

Silence.

I stood a moment, then moved back to where Ranger lay. To my surprise, he was on his feet, but wavering unsteadily. I reached both arms under him to hoist him up and carry him to my room, but he cried out again and I realized from the wetness it was his chest that was hurt. Returning him to the ground, I found he could stand on his own, and he could move, so I let him limp behind me to my door, entered, then risked an oil lamp.

He was creased across the chest, a ¾-inch deep wound that was bleeding freely. I grabbed a sheet off my bunk, tore it into strips, stuffed the wound and bound him, making the rest of it and one of my blankets into a bed for him next to the potbelly stove. He plopped down, and although the binding was quickly soaked through, the bleeding seemed to be controlled.

"Stay," I told him, then hustled back to the McGregor's kitchen, where I found the situation well under control. By the light of a shaded candle McGregor had bound the man's hands behind his back with a clothesline, tight enough that his hands had gone white, and he was still unmoving on the kitchen floor, although bleeding from two cuts where the heavy revolver had creased his noggin.

"Well done," I said. Realizing for the first time I was shirtless, hardly fittin' in front of a lady, I apologized and backed out of the kitchen door.

"I'll be back, soon as I'm decent," I said, my face turning a little red as I could feel the heat of it.

In moments, after again checking on Ranger and filling a pail of water to sit beside his makeshift bed, I was dressed and re-entered the dimly lit kitchen, returning McGregor's shotgun to the rack over the door.

The man was beginning to come around. I did not recognize him, but I jerked him up and sat him in a kitchen chair, his back to the wall. A piece of the clothesline still lay nearby, so I bound him to the chair. He was still not focusing, so I walked to the sink, pumped a coffee cup full of water, and returned, flinging it in his face.

That brought him around, but covered Maddy's

floor with bloody water. "Sorry," I said, but she dismissed it.

"Who are you?" I demanded.

He eyed me carefully, and seemed to get his wits about him. Merely shaking his head, he ignored the question, a little on the haughty side, I thought. I'd cure that.

I reached over and gave him a hard finger flick to the spot on his head where he could use a few stitches, and he winced and cursed.

"I said, who are you?"

"President Grant," he said, a lazy smile crossing his face. He was a brindle top redhead, red laced with blond salted with a little gray, with a wide baby face full of ruddy freckles that made him look younger and less of a threat than most would figure him to be. But he was sun-browned, prairie wind burned, and had been ridden hard many times in his life. His hands were like claws, and scared from hard work, probably breaking rocks in a territorial pen. I wasn't fooled by the baby face.

I eyed him, my hand on the butt of the .44, thinking I'd bust those smart lips wide open, then glanced up to see Maddy looking as if she was slightly in shock. Seeing his bloodied teeth scatter across her kitchen floor would likely put her over the edge, so I resisted the temptation.

I sighed deeply. "I don't imagine you'd like to return to your covers, Miss Maddy?"

Her back went rigid, and she snapped to attention. "So you can beat this poor creature into submission."

I couldn't help but chuckle. "Should he be any more in submission, I believe we'd have to plant him out in the garden."

"Nonetheless, please just do your job as a lawman should."

"You've a short memory, Miss Maddy," I snapped, a little harsher than I probably should have, as she was still wide eyed and a little slack-jawed. I eased my tone. "Wasn't he just holding a large caliber firearm on you and your father, in the dark of night? I'd suppose he was uninvited?"

"Damn sure was," her father stepped in. "Maddy, you need some sleep. Go on now. Tag will handle this."

"I'm sorry," she said, to my surprise. "This has all been a little too much for me."

"I'll tie this one up in the barn, and take him in with the sun. You folks don't worry, things are under control."

"Was that Ranger I heard yelping?" Maddy asked. "Ranger doesn't seem one to yelp."

"It was, he took a shot across his chest bone, but I

think he'll mend. He's at rest in my room, not that he favors being inside."

"Anything I can do?" she asked.

"I'll leave him here tomorrow, and you can watch him if you're a mind to."

"It'll be my pleasure. When I looked out my window at the commotion, he had a man by the leg, going at him like a crocodile, and the man was screaming as if a lion trap had him." She shook her head. "He may have saved us all, and I'll get him well, God willing." I gave her a reassuring smile, and after a shuddering sigh, she continued. "I'll take your advice and find my covers."

I removed the line binding the brindle top to the chair, jerked him to his feet, and headed out, stopping to turn back to McGregor. "I'll borrow your line if you don't mind."

"You can tie him in the feed room, if you'd like, and the door bars on the outside."

"That'll do." I nodded and shoved my prisoner out into the night.

He stumbled toward the barn, but I redirected him to my room, shoving him inside hard enough that he hit the floor with a thump, greeted by a low rumble from Ranger, who'd lost a good deal of blood but little of his attitude.

Following brindle top in, I greeted him with the

toe of my boot deep in his gut. He upchucked right there on my floor.

"Well, that was a damn bad idea," I said, now having a bit of a mess to clean up. He moaned in response.

"You're gonna tell me your name and all your particulars," I said, my tone a warning. I crossed to my bed, gathered my half-saber out of its scabbard, and returned to the man, letting the light catch on the blade as I showed it to him.

"This blade has been in the gullet of more than one ass-eyed hooligan, from Gettysburg to Shiloh, so don't for a second think I won't split you from asshole to elbow."

"You're a lawman. You won't do that."

I moved around behind him, put a boot on his neck, and reached down and sawed off the top half inch of his right ear.

## Chapter Sixteen

HE SCREAMED like a pair of mating bald eagles, loud enough to pain my ears. Moving back around, I could see the whites of his eyes around both pupils as he whimpered. I showed him the top of his ear just as Reverend McGregor slung my door aside.

"Thought you were taking him to the grain room?" he asked. I figured I was in for one hell of a biblical lecture.

"Shortly. I believe he's ready to get some rest... soon as we finish our conversation."

"I don't want to find his head on a fence post, come morning," McGregor said, then added, "like the last one."

I smiled. The old boy was smarter than he looked and maybe tougher, under his slightly frayed nightshirt with boney knees showing, than one might think.

"I'll try not, if I can contain myself. That one was stinking so bad after a week with the crows having et his eyeballs, I could barely stand to bury the damn thing."

That seemed to be all it took, his voice quivered as he spilled all. "My name is Fred…Alfred Phillips, I'm from Washoe Meadows, over near the Sierra, Sacramento before that. I come into town just day before yesterday, riding a freight car, and took up with some fellas who said they had a rough job of work to do and was paying five dollars the day, and would provide me with a mount for the duration. Shit fire man, I'm just a'passin' through."

"What fellas?" I asked.

"Same ones I rode in here with."

"That's not an answer," I said, flashing the saber blade at him again. "I guess you'd favor matching ear stubs?"

"I swear. All I know is one was named Liam and another, a greaser, named Enrico."

"There seemed to be more than three of you."

"I didn't catch the names of the other two, but they was riding the rails just like me."

"You ever heard of the Lazy Snake?"

"No, sir. Don't know nothing about no snakes. Just that I don't like the slimy things. These fellas were camped out of town a ways, that's all I know, except they said they had a fella to put toes up, a bad fella who needed the killin', and should it happen, we'd get another double eagle then could be on our way."

I jerked him up, sat him in one of my two spindle backed chairs, and bound his head wound with a length of the flannel sheet tight enough to stop the bleeding, then I hauled him next door and with his hands still bound behind him, shoved him in the grain room, bound his ankles with a lead rope, and barred the door, hoping one of those snakes he so disliked would take a mind to gnaw on him. Grain bins always were the worst place for snakes, attracted by the mice and rats.

I bid McGregor good night, shoved a chair under my doorknob, laid my .44 on the chest next to my bunk, gave Ranger a final check of his bandages and a scratch on the ears, then bedded down.

I didn't think they'd be back, so I slept the sleep of the innocent.

Dawn found me trying to figure out just who and how many came to visit us in the night. Judging by the track, it had been five just as ol' earless brindle top had claimed.

The tracks came in from the north, and I figured later I'd backtrack them and see where they'd come from. So far, I'd stayed close to the place, figuring that they'd tied their stock up out in the sage and come in on foot. Two of them had stayed back with three of the horses, two had come in leading their mounts, tied them a ways out, then come to my door, and one, afoot all the way to the house. I guess they got a surprise when they opened my door, and Ranger came at them from the side. Judging by the length of his strides, one had set out like Lucifer was on his tail, and the other had been waylaid by Ranger. He and the dog had rolled around a bit until he got off a shot, then he lit out after his partner.

The next surprise made my day. A Mexican, with bandoliers of cartridges crisscrossing his chest and a fine Winchester laying a couple of body lengths away, was on his back, still barely breathing, a hundred paces from the barn. One of my off-thrown .44 shots had taken him low and left in the back. Pure luck as I was firing at phantoms. The good Lord has a way about him....

I tried to roust him but it wouldn't happen.

By the time I returned to the barn, the reverend was feeding his stock.

"I see your prisoner is still among the grain bins."

"Good, but we've got another one, and this one needs the doc. Seems he caught a stray shot while out enjoying the night air. A real pity."

"The devil was at work last night. Should I hitch up the grain wagon?"

"Yes, sir. If you don't mind, I'll keep on judging the situation. See what more I can find."

"Maddy has the coffee made, biscuits in the oven, and is frying up some side pork."

"Maybe you'd better get me a cup...."

"No, she'll be glad to see you. Seems she'd rather have you about than some roughneck with a gun shoved in her face."

I smiled. "Then I'll fetch a cup and go on with my detective work."

I knocked softly on the kitchen door, and she stuck her head out. This time her hair was fixed, hanging long to the middle of her back.

"Sleep well?" she asked, a slightly impish smile on her lovely face.

"A little on the toss and turn and wake up every fifteen minute side, to tell the truth."

"Will a cup of coffee help?"

"You bet. We got another lowlife to tend to, how-some-ever. He's out in the sage and your father is hitching up to take him to town. You might consider the ride in, as this Mexican caballero won't ride easy, and might not make it...and I'm not sure you ought to be here alone."

She looked as serious as an honest woman could, but went ahead and fetched me a cup. While she was pouring, I added, "I think it wise if I find another place to bunk. Seems trouble follows me like lobos riding drag on a herd."

She paused and seemed to think on that a moment, then turned to me, brow furrowed. "You ride in here, bring us a hogshead of trouble, then want to ride out and leave us to fend off the wolves?"

"I just thought—"

"Well don't think. You stick around here in case there's more trouble."

"Yes, ma'am."

I took my coffee and started away, and she called out, "You be back here in fifteen minutes and there's side pork, biscuits, gravy, and a dollop of homemade apple butter."

"My pleasure, but we might ought to eat on the trail, as this fellow out in the sage don't look to have too much time."

"Should I come with you?" she asked.

"Nothing to do but haul him to the doc."

We got him loaded onto the bed of the grain wagon, but he didn't last through the effort, and was going cold by the time McGregor got it turned in the brush and back to the house.

The reverend paused before dismounting the seat and said a quiet prayer. I had my own thoughts on what I'd pray for the lowlife, but kept them to myself. If he was the Mexican known as Enrico Zaragosa, who Angel had told me was the Lazy Snake Mexican rider and who was known as Rico to his chums, then I was another step closer climbing the ladder of revenge.

It was polite of Rico to give up the ghost before we sat out to town, as it allowed us to sit around a table to breakfast, albeit a little glum on the McGregor's part as there was a stiffening Mexican just outside the kitchen door. As for me, it was all I could do not to break out in song.

We saved enough for brindle top, Alfred, I guess he said was his handle, and I untied him and allowed him to eat, but I hoped doing so while under the gun would give him indigestion. Then I stoutly retied him for the trip to town.

We were a sight, Reverend McGregor in frock coat and top hat with the traces, Maddy, at his side in a simple yellow calico dress and matching bonnet; Alfred with a bloody head bandage, the Mexican cadaver with a flat wide-brimmed hat resting on his chest—I'd removed the bandoliers as they held forty rounds for my new Yellow Boy —and Ranger, swaddled in a bloody wrap, all in the back of the grain wagon. And me astride Dusty, with an all but brand new 1866 Yellow Boy King's Improved Winchester in the scabbard under my knee. About the only thing good I can say about ol' Rico, the boy took good care of his weapons.

I was beginning to like town. Since leaving lots

of possessions behind in my Salmon country cabin, I'd acquired even more.

For the first time, I was to meet Dr. Simon Ironsmith, who I was to learn was the barber, Isaac Ironsmith's brother, and whose office was in his fairly new house on the west end of town. I found it a little strange that Isaac had talked about damn near everything under the sun, but had not mentioned that his brother was the only doctor, dentist, and undertaker in the territory. Simon, too, was tall and white haired, but without the rosy red alcoholic nose. Which I found to be a good trait for a physician to fight shy of.

He sprinkled a little alcohol on Alfred's ear stub, which I quickly informed him was not the reason for the visit, and dressed it properly with a patch, then looked at Ranger's chest wound, which was the reason we'd darkened his door. Informing me it was too late to stitch anything up, and that he wasn't a dog doc but was happy as the dog seemed to have saved some human lives, he complimented me on stuffing the wound, said to watch out for proud flesh, and sent us on our way. We left the Mexican in Doc Ironside's care, overpaid him with a ten dollar gold piece from Rico's pocket—I doubt now if he'll turn any dogs down as patients—and I excused myself for my office.

Reverend McGregor was happy to accept half

the other thirty Rico had in his pocket, saying the devil would hate to see Rico's money go to doing the Lord's work, and anything the devil hated was just fine with him. The McGregor's headed to Mayor Pointer's store for supplies. I planned to head there later myself, and was smiling as I could pay with Rico's gold, and Rico wasn't so *rico* anymore.

It was still yet to reach nine o'clock in the morning, when I knew Natchez Pete's trial was to begin, so, after depositing Alfred in a cell, I headed for the Mystic Palace.

Judge Thorne was in the parlor sipping what I presumed to be coffee and reading a Leslie's Illustrated, and I took the liberty of joining him. The Mystic had been built by a retired Whaler, who I had learned was back in Mystic, Connecticut. The place was fancy as railroad towns go, and even had a small restaurant, but catered to guests only, so I'd avoided it. Judge Thorne was a guest.

"Tag, you like a little tea?"

"Never developed the taste for the stuff. Not enough bones in it for me."

"Coffee then?"

"Yes, sir."

He yelled and a Chinaman appeared, and hustled away to fill the judge's wishes.

"I figured you'd be at the church?" The trial was

to be held there as it was the only place in town with enough seating.

"Trial's put off. Still have a couple of witnesses who haven't showed up yet."

"Good, then you might like to do me a favor?"

"Which is…?" he asked, showing a little interest.

"You know that law abiding rancher you're always bragging on?"

He knew exactly who I meant, but played dumb. "I don't brag on any rancher I know of, Tag."

"Colonel Dillon, who you say is not above the law."

He gave me a cold stare, and when I didn't back down, spat out, "God damn it, Slade, you do that just to rile me? A hell of a way to ask a favor."

I smiled a little sheepishly. "You're right, judge. It's just that these old boys who think they own the country, and the law, and even the free graze, get my goat."

He seemed to calm down a little, so I continued. "I want to take a ride out to the Lazy Snake and have a chat with the Colonel."

"He'll be in town next Sunday for church."

"Too long. I think I need to have this chat while things are fresh in my mind."

"What things?"

The Chinaman arrived with my coffee, so I waited for him to leave.

"How about him sending his boys to shoot me down in my bed?"

"The hell you say, I don't think Dillon—"

"I just delivered another of his boys to the digger, and another newly hired hand to jail."

"Who?"

"Who what?"

"Who went to the digger?"

"Lucky shot from my Army Colt put down a Mexican. Rico, I think he was called."

"You know this Mexican to be Rico, Dillon's man?"

"Nope, but I can't think of anyone else who's on the prod for me. They came right out to McGregor's, held them at gunpoint, shot my dog, and I'm sure had intent to fill me full of lead."

"Let me finish my tea and my newspaper, and we'll go take a look at this Mexican. I know most of Dillon's men, by sight at least."

"Fine. I got a few things to pick up at Pointers, then I'll walk you down."

I started out and was stopped by the judge's voice. "Slade, I have no reason to think Dillon is on the prod for you, to use your words. Just because you had a row with Cavanaugh—"

"Twice, with the scum who's supposed to be Dillon's shooter—"

"Who said that? Cavanaugh is a cowhand now, no matter his past."

"And I'm Saint Peter and you're President Grant."

"There you go again, Slade. Don't be smart." Then he laughed, and added, "And how come you're a saint and I'm a mere president?"

I laughed as well, but continued on point. "He's a shooter, if a damn dumb one, and Toole was Dillon's man."

The judge got serious again. "That was over him cheating at cards. It had nothing to do with Dillon."

"Seems to me there's a common thread showing up here. So you think that bunch who showed up last night just came for tea?"

"Alright, alright. You go run your errand, I'll finish my tea and paper, and we'll go see if this Mexican is really Dillon's man."

"Then you can visit the man I have in jail, who was with them last night, and then we can take a ride out to see this law abiding cattleman?"

"If it's like you say it is, we can."

I don't know why I should, but I'm looking forward to going right into the hornet's nest, and seeing the look on Dillon's face when I'm on his own porch. I doubt if he'll try anything with the judge along, but I'll bet the temerity of my actions that he'll consider it a royal insult, will prod him into getting a little reckless—and I want them coming after me, for

I have a plan. He's damn sure irritated and out of sorts already, as I'm sure the rider who accompanied Rico to the McGregor's was ol' scar face Willy Stark, as one of the horses was shy a right rear shoe. And he would have ridden straight back to the Lazy Snake to report the fact he'd left Rico in the brush, probably thinking him dead.

And I am pleased that his mistake turned out to be true. Two down, one out of commission again, maybe forever as that boot heel to the ribcage, with any luck, drove a rib splinter through a lung. Things are looking up.

Should be an interesting afternoon.

## Chapter Seventeen

THE JUDGE SEEMED SHOCKED to the core when he saw Rico, pennies on his eyes, in the pine box which Doc Ironsmith had already had delivered.

"No need to talk to the other fella," Thorne said. "This is Dillon's man, and if you want me to ride out there with you, let's head for Pettibone's and get Phinias to rig up a buggy. I'm not riding one of those crowbaits he rents out."

Leaving Dusty with Phinias and placing my new Winchester on the floor of the buggy, I joined Judge Thorne to ride in style out to the Snake.

It was a thirty minute trot to the Lazy Snake headquarters, twenty five of it on the ranch. I'd been told the place was in excess of a hundred thousand acres, and have no reason to doubt.

A cowhand in a field not more than a mile from

the house spotted us and rode over close enough to see faces, then without even a wave whipped up his pony and pounded away toward ranch headquarters.

And the last half mile to the headquarters was imposing. The lane was lined with poplars and the last quarter mile of the fences were flat board, whitewashed, as were all the outbuildings...even the privies to serve the barn and bunkhouse and one smaller house I figured to be that of a foreman gleamed sparkling white in the sun.

The house itself was two storied with a pair of full grown elms in its front yard, and I guessed the colonel had been impressed by the plantations in the south, which he'd obviously taken note of before he put the torch to them. Six well-milled columns rose across the front; were I a student of Roman or Greek architecture I'd venture a guess as to their design origin. He was a man who appreciated the finer things, as I should have surmised by the silk shirts and diamond stickpin.

As we approached the hitching rail, a few feet in front of a white picket fence that enclosed the house, some of the local scum began to gather up behind, a few of them with work gloves, a few with bare hands and side arms ready for blood work, should it come to that. Arms folded in front of them were indications of our welcome. I felt like a laying hen trying to disguise myself as a chick in a golden eagle's nest.

"He's a humble sort, ain't he?" I said to the judge, who didn't bother to answer.

No one greeted us or said a word as we dismounted the buggy and walked up the pavement stones to the wide stairway leading to the railed porch. I could feel the judge's palpable discomfort, and smiled inwardly. Maybe he was beginning to understand that Dillon was little more than a tyrant who, as I had suggested often, thought himself above the law.

I stopped short when I recognized Willy Stark— hard to miss with the ugly scar bisecting his cheek— and I pulled up short. "Hey, Willy."

He looked a little stupid for a moment, then answered from five deep in the crowd. "Yeah."

"You get that rear shoe fixed yet?"

"What rear shoe?"

"The one your sorrel is missing. You got to be careful with something like that. Folks will know where you been and what you been doing."

He reddened in the face, but said no more, and I mounted the stairs.

I rapped on the door, a little louder than might seem polite.

It quickly swung aside.

"Good afternoon, Chang," the judge, who'd snatched his hat off a little too deferentially for my taste, said to the Chinese gentleman who stood politely aside and waved us in.

"Gentleman of house...dressing," Chang said, and led us into a sitting room, where a pot of hot coffee already rested, steaming on a side table, along with three cups. The rider had wasted no time informing them of the coming "guests."

Chang poured a cup for each of us, offered sugar and cream which the judge accepted, then disappeared.

It was ten minutes before Dillon strode in, dressed in soft wool pants, moccasins, and a smoking jacket over a silk shirt. The bulge at his side told me he was heeled, and I suspected a gambler's pistol in a pocket of the jacket...he expected me, all right.

"What brings you fellas this far out in the country?" he asked, shaking hands with the judge, ignoring me, and taking a seat across the room.

"Seems the marshal here had a little trouble last night," the judge offered, sipping his coffee.

I heard the front door close softly, and saw Shank Cavanaugh and another Lazy Snake rider, a young blond fella with fine features, cross in front of the doorway, and heard the scraping of chair legs on the polished entry floor. Obviously, they were backup in case things got a little out of hand in the parlor.

"How so?" Dillon asked, and walked over and

poured himself a cup, giving an irritated look at the door where Chang had disappeared.

"Tell him," the judge said, directing his command to me.

"Some might think it trouble. I thought of it as getting rid of some scum."

"How so?" Dillon asked again.

"Five fellas, two of them Lazy Snake riders for sure, came calling in the black of night. One of them caught a slug in the back, one of the ones they accompanied, is in my jail, Stark's right outside, he was one of the scum suckin' pigs, and the other two are most likely cowering out in your bunkhouse, or somewhere hereabout, and someone's been pickin' buckshot out of one ol' boy's backside."

Dillon's eyes narrowed and his mouth became a tight line before he finally spoke.

"Are you accusing Lazy Snake riders of something illegal? I fired Rico Zaragosa yesterday—"

"I didn't say who it was," I said, smiling a little too broadly.

"He's the only Lazy Snake rider missing," Dillon snapped.

"So, you've got a hundred thousand or so acres and a half-dozen range shacks and you know where every man is?"

"I run this ranch, Slade, and yes, I know where every man is."

"And I guess you had supper with all the boys last night?"

He turned to Thorne. "Are you part of this inquisition, judge?"

"I rode out here with the marshal as he seemed to think it might not be safe for him to come alone."

Dillon guffawed. "Damn sure wouldn't, he comes here accusing me and my men. I'd have him horse-whipped right now, were you not here."

"Thanks, judge," I said, ignoring the colonel, "as I'd hate to have to put a bunch of ugly Lazy Snake boys in the ground, should they try and take a whip to me."

"Humph," the colonel managed, then turned to the judge. "The fact is," Dillon said, "we took delivery on a new bull yesterday, General Napoleon, a pure bred Aberdeen angus, an angus doddie, long of loin and weather resistant, all the way from back east. Bred by Ian MacTavish. I'd called all the boys in from the range to take place in the celebration. All but Enrico Zaragosa, who I fired day before yesterday."

"I guess it would be impolite to drink a fella's coffee and call him a liar."

"Damned impolite, and damned dangerous," he said, fire in his eyes.

But I kept it up. "You said, just a few minutes ago, you fired Rico yesterday, not day before yesterday. You having trouble keeping your facts straight, Dillon?"

He sputtered, but merely glared.

"Long of loin, eh?" I said. "Sounds like expensive hamburger."

"More than you'll make in a lifetime, Slade," he snapped. "Now get the hell out of my home."

"Tough country, hope he makes it," I said. A casual smile crossed my face, which seemed to infuriate the Colonel even more.

"You son-of-a-bitch, don't you threaten me or mine, and no man calls me a liar." He was on his feet, red in the face, his hand in the pocket of his smoking jacket. I lay a hand casually on the butt of my Army Colt, hoping he'd pull the pistol and not try my shoot-through-the-pocket trick.

Cavanaugh and his cohort appeared in the doorway, but their iron was still holstered.

"Enough," Thorne snapped, also rising. "So, you deny any of your men were involved in this incident at the McGregor's'?"

"You know better than to even ask that insulting question, judge," Dillon said, spittle flying.

"Well, he has spoken," I said, rising at the same time, stressing the *he* as if it was the Lord to whom I was referring.

"Thanks for the coffee, Colonel," I said.

"Thank Chang," he said, "had I been sure it was you, he could have saved the grounds."

"Somehow, had you been sure it was me, I think it would have been rat poison," I guffawed, and it seemed to irritate him even more, but his hand was out of the pocket.

"Come again, judge," he said, ignoring me, "and leave this son-of-a-bitch in town." Then he turned to me. "Don't let the door hit you in the ass on your way out, Slade. And don't be caught on Lazy Snake property ever again. Soon as you cross the line back into town don't ever head back. You'll be shot for a trespasser you darken my door again."

"Damn, and the coffee was right fine. Thank Chang for me." As I headed for the door, I said to the judge who was trailing behind, loud enough that Dillon could hear. "And you thought old man Dillon didn't think he was above the law. What do you think now?"

I pushed between Cavanaugh and the other fella, and got a good look at him for the first time. He was blue eyed, much the same eyes as Colonel Dillon had, only the Colonels were cold and icy, and this boy's seemed wide and inquiring. I'll bet he's the colonel's nephew, who Lizzy had mentioned. I was hoping to get a chance to give Dillon's shooter another poke in the ribs, but he covered up and stepped back. I guess he'd had enough of me and his rib cage clashing.

I laughed again, and shoved my way through the front door, with Thorne on my tail, which was a good thing as now the rest of the riders had gathered and some of them carried long arms, including a double barrel coach gun or two.

We mounted up, I snatched up the Winchester, and the judge quickly shook the traces and headed for the poplar-lined lane. I kept an eye over my shoulder, not wanting to take a Winchester slug between my shoulder blades. Dillon seemed to have forgotten his manners, and hadn't accompanied us out.

"Well, that was fine as a light spring rain...just fine," the judge said.

I laughed. "About like I thought it would go. You'd have probably gotten a supper invite, had I not been along."

"And you'd probably had gotten horsewhipped, had I not been along."

"Odds are it would have gone worse than that for me. I owe you supper, for all the trouble."

"Got to prepare for trial tomorrow, presuming my witnesses came in on the train, but I'll let you owe me."

"Done. So who was the other fella, the young fella, out in the hall with Cavanaugh?"

"Seth somebody. Another of the Lazy Snake riders."

"Carried his six shooter mighty low on the hip for a cowhand."

The judge shrugged. "That's all I know about him, except...the fact is, he's Dillon's nephew, why?"

"Just a'wonderin'," I said, shrugging. Dillon's nephew, now that was a revelation, or would have been had Lizzy not filled me in.

"What's he doing here," I asked, not quite ready to drop the subject.

"Like I said, I don't know much about him. Seems like a nice young man. His mother, Dillon's youngest sister, sent him out for a year or so before he goes to college."

"How long's he been here?"

"Most of a year, I guess."

So he would have been here when they rode on my sister's place. She named him in her journal as only "Seth" but as being there before, and old Ignacio named him as being in the bunch who did the heinous deed, so he was on the list. Young or no.

"So, what now?" the judge asked.

I was quiet for a long moment, wondering how much I could actually trust the judge. Finally, I said, "Well, I guess that's up to the Lazy Snake boys. I don't believe for one minute that Rico was there on his own. What the hell did he have to gain putting me in the ground? He was there on the behest of Dillon or Cavanaugh, who I shamed. And probably Dillon as I suspect Cavanaugh would want the pleasure of taking his own revenge. Nope, it's Dillon at the end of that trail."

"Why Dillon?"

"Why would Dillon want me dead?" I figured I'd said enough, so I shrugged. "Don't like my good looks is about all I can surmise. Or maybe he don't like me being so near to Maddy McGregor?"

"Dillon and Maddy, not likely. She's a preacher's daughter. Dillon would have his sights set a lot higher."

"McGregor acts like a man of substance, and man of property. I figure him to be a preacher man because he had the calling, not because he needs the money."

"Nope. His family were Maryland folks, sympathetic to the South, and got burned out and had their stock—several hundred head of bald face Scottish Highland cattle and a hundred head of prime horse flesh—run off at the time. He came west poor as a church mouse."

"Then why?" I asked, innocently.

"That makes no sense a'tall," the judge said, and pulled the horse down from a trot to a brisk walk to give her a bit of a blow.

"Life don't," I said.

"Don't what?" the judge asked.

"Don't make much sense a'tall," I said, but I was thinking about my next move, and my next move involved those two bear traps I'd hauled all the way from the Salmon country.

The judge returned the buggy, then headed for the Mystic Palace and I gathered up Dusty and headed for my office.

I was convinced of one thing: Dillon would send his dogs after me, and this time he would make sure I didn't walk away to trouble him again.

But next time, I'd be waiting. Sneak up on me once, I'm a fool, sneak up on me twice and you're a damned fool, and if I have my way, the Lazy Snake boys will be dead damn fools.

## Chapter Eighteen

TO MY SURPRISE, Angel's brother, young Ignacio, awaited, squatted down on his haunches, when I tied up in front of the office. Wentworth and Shorty both had mounts at the rail outside the office, so, being hungry myself and not eager to trade barbs, I asked the boy, "When did you last eat?"

"Early this morning, at Señor Henderson's, before light, I had a hunk of cheese and bread before I walked in."

It was twenty miles to the Henderson place. And it was already damn near quitting time for most folks. "How about I treat you to an early supper?"

"As you wish, Señor, but it is my brother...."

"What's wrong?"

"Nothing, Señor. He is up in the hills, across the

tracks, and wishes to speak with you. He could not come in town."

"Good, let's eat and we'll take him something."

"As you wish."

I walked around to Natchez Pete's cell window to see if the prisoners had eaten, not wanting to run into Wentworth as I was not up to taking any lip from the big sheriff, and maybe having to give him a fat one. To my surprise, I found not a barred window, but a ragged hole you could ride a horse through.

"Wait over at Sally's," I instructed Iggy, and headed back to the front door.

Wentworth, Shorty, John Pointer, and Isaac Ironsmith were having a confab when I walked in.

"Good job, Slade," Wentworth snapped as soon as I closed the door behind me.

"Thanks," I said, sarcastically, "what did I do?"

"Ain't what you did, it's what you didn't do. You didn't watch your prisoners—"

"Suddenly they're my prisoners?" I asked, and guffawed a little. "Seems you've been claiming them."

"Whose ever they are, one of them escaped."

"By the look of the wall around the side, he had a little help."

"How'd you know—?"

"Hole you could drive a freight wagon through. You thought I wouldn't notice?"

"Where were you, marshal?" Pointer asked.

"Doing business, mayor, that's where."

"That's not an answer," he said, accusingly.

"I was out at the Lazy Snake with Judge Thorne. I didn't know I had to give an hourly report to the town council."

"I didn't mean—" Pointer said, rather sheepishly.

"As you probably know, there's another dead man over at the docs, awaiting planting, and he was a Lazy Snake rider. Seems fittin' I'd asked the herd bull out there about what his riders were doing calling on the town marshal, the preacher, and the preacher's daughter, in the dead of night."

Wentworth quickly changed the subject, a little too quickly for my taste. "We've got to get a posse up to run this Natchez Pete Pelletier and his boys down."

"How many were there?" I asked John Pointer as I was already feeling like putting a boot up Wentworth's backside.

"Two more. They rented a freight wagon and four dray horses from Phinias, bought some heavy line from me, rode right around the back of the jail, tied off to the bars, and whipped up the team. One of them had come inside and tied Shorty here to his chair—"

"It's my chair," Wentworth said, and got a glare from Pointer, who then turned his attention back to me.

"Damn nigh jerked the whole damn building down. They had three riding horses tied out back. Left the freight wagon there, and hightailed it south into the hills."

"So, it's good job 'Shorty,' right?" I couldn't help but smile at Wentworth, who was fuming, so I continued to prod him. "Posse is a good idea, Sheriff. Unless he's hiding here in the city, I guess that's your bailiwick."

"So, you're not riding with us?"

"I got a town to tend to," I said, and both Pointer and the barber, Ironsmith, eyed me like a bull at a bastard calf. I guess they were beginning to have their doubts. But I was in no mind to kowtow to them as I had other fences to mend.

"Go get 'em, sheriff," I said, "I got other business," and with that I walked out and headed for Sally's.

He yelled after me, "When I get them, and I will, the reward goes to me, Slade. You're out of the cut."

"Then go earn it," I said.

Iggy and I wolfed some stew down, got two jars full and I took one over to Alfred, who was still securely in his cell across the hall from the newly ventilated one. Wentworth and the other three had disappeared, I suppose to round up a posse.

"Thanks," Alfred said. "It's gonna get a little chilly in here tonight with that hole in the wall."

"You're tough." I opened the cell door to where a pile of rubble covered Natchez Pete's blanket, shook it out, and shoved it through to Alfred, which doubled his supply. "That'll keep you till we can get some masons to work on the wall."

"How about a cup of coffee?" Alfred asked.

"Stew's got enough liquid and I'm in a hurry. Be happy you got that," I said, and headed for the office.

"I ain't complaining 'bout that," he said, then added, "What's gonna become of me?"

"You'll probably hang," I said, just for pure meanness. I left him shouting, hopefully with indigestion, loaded young Iggy up behind my saddle, and rode across the tracks and up into the hills.

We found Angel and my mule, Jackson, about a mile back from the rails.

"What are you doing to avenge my father?" he asked, without so much as a hello.

I pulled the jar of stew from my saddle bags and handed it over. As he ate, I filled him in.

"There's two of them cold as stone, one in the ground and one about to be."

Between chews, he accused, "You are leaving me out of this. It is my fight as well, and I will fight with you or fight alone."

I thought about it a minute, then decided. "Okay,

here's the plan. Two draws to the east you'll find a barranca with a little water in it. A quarter mile below the spring that feeds that trickle you'll find a wind cave halfway up the hillside, and in there are some traps and some weapons...."

In moments, I was on my way to the McGregor's, Iggy to hole up in my old cave where I'd stashed some edibles, then to head back to Henderson's herd and the sheep he was supposed to be tending in the high meadow, and Angel to find the traps and my weapons and haul them to my place at the McGregor's. We had work to do, and it was work better done in dark of night.

I didn't much favor the idea of young Angel helping in my quest, but he was determined, and I figured better have him where I can keep an eye on him than face a bevy of Lazy Snake riders by himself.

After tying Dusty in the barn and making peace with Ranger and checking his wound, I walked to the McGregor's back door. The preacher answered with shotgun in hand.

"You're a little more cautious these days?" I said, with a smile.

"A darn sight more cautious," he said, and stood aside and waved me in. "Lord takes care of them who takes care of themselves," he added.

Maddy already had a coffee cup in hand and was

pouring. Something in a pair of pots on the stove smelled mighty good, but I was still full to the brim from the stew.

"You eaten?" Maddy asked.

"I have, early supper." I went on to suggest they ride in to spend the night at the hotel or find friends to bunk with for the night, but they'd have none of it.

Finally, I fessed up. "I think we'll have company again tonight. Seems I got ol' Colonel Dillon in a bit of a tizzy earlier today. I can't imagine him not sending his boys to call on us again...on me, I mean. Only this time, it'll not be some stumble-bums from the tracks. This time it may just be his whole crew."

"We'll stay here, and with the good Lord's help, we'll watch over what's ours."

Maddy seemed to puff up. "Mace wouldn't hurt either of us, Taggart. He might have a bone to pick with you, but I doubt even that."

I smiled a little sadly at her. "So, you don't think he had anything to do with those fellas who came in the dark of night."

"No, I don't."

So I ignored her, and turned to her father. "I wish you would have let me move out," I offered again.

"Too late now," Maddy said, "even if you could

have convinced us, and you couldn't...but that doesn't mean I think Mace had a thing to do—"

"Then stay down. I don't think they'll try and burn us out, but I don't know, so keep some buckets at hand in case they sling torches through the windows. And I'm sure there will be plenty of lead flying, so stay low when you hear that first shot. They'll do whatever is necessary to put me down. So..."

"So?" Maddy asked.

"So I won't be where they'll think I'll be. I won't be in my room, I'll be out in the brush, or God knows where. Will you keep Ranger in the house with you?"

"Of course," she said.

"He'll try and help out, and he's in no condition...."

"I'll keep him inside with me. But he's lots better already, eating and moving about."

"Yes, thank you, I checked on him. Within the hour a young friend of mine will be here--"

"A young friend?" Maddy asked.

"Angel Sanchez."

"The boy who escaped from jail."

"He didn't escape, I let him free."

"But didn't he—"

"He did nothing but ask about the death of his father. He made the mistake of asking with gun in hand."

"But didn't his father—"

"Maddy, his father was a fine man, who'd worked for my sister for a long while. She adored the man."

"Your sister?" She looked totally confused.

"My sister and her husband and their two daughters were on the Bar M."

"I knew Sarah and Jake and the girls well, fine church going...But I didn't know she had a brother. I was sickened by the accident..."

"It was no accident. The McIntosh family was murdered by Colonel Dillon and his bunch from the Lazy Snake."

"I don't believe that," she said, looking shocked.

"Believe it or not, that's what happened. I'll let you read Sarah's journal, and you can make up your own mind. Dillon wanted to buy them out and they wouldn't sell. He wanted the water on the place, thought he had to have it."

"I can't believe that about Mace. He wouldn't...."

"You just stay low when the shooting starts, or better go on into town."

"We'll stay down," Reverend McGregor said. "Won't we, Maddy?" he said, and she shook her head, seemingly in a bit of a daze. But then he turned to me, and seemed to sober. "I don't believe Mace Dillon has a damn thing to do with this."

I wondered then, maybe Colonel Dillon had no

intentions toward Maddy McGregor, but maybe Maddy McGregor had intentions toward Mace Dillon? And maybe Preacher McGregor had aspirations for this beautiful daughter?

I left them and reconnoitered around the place for a couple hundred yards on all sides. The last time they had come in on the road, but had tied most of their mounts almost two hundred yards distant from the house and barn. The way it had looked to me, only Stark and Rico had led their mounts nearby. There was a stand of smoke trees there, with places to tie horses. I had no reason to believe they wouldn't do the same this time. They hadn't proved themselves to be much in the way of military tacticians.

There was a game and cattle trail almost wide enough to ride horses side by side leading from the copse of trees to the house. At least some of them would come that way, others might circle the house to make sure I didn't escape. The colonel was a military man, who might take more of an interest this go-round, and he would make sure they flank me. I figured them for a half-dozen or more men again, only this time all Lazy Snake riders, those riders who were gunfighters more than cowhands. So the odds were bad, at best.

And I'd bet that Cavanaugh and Dillon would not be with them. Cavanaugh was still too laid up to be much good, particularly horseback. And Dillon wouldn't soil his hands with this kind of dirty work.

There was no doubt in my mind that even if I was able to take Seth Rheinhart, Tate Jorgensen, Willy Stark, and the Indian, Crooked Arm, down this night, my work wouldn't be over by a damn sight. I still had the head of the snake to sever, and his right arm.

I'd started out thinking I had six to bury, had taken care of two, and still had six to bury. I hoped to make some actual headway this night.

When I got back to my room, Angel arrived at the same time, leading Jackson who had a full load of traps and weapons aboard.

"Water," Angel asked, and I poured him a mug from my bone white pitcher which rested on the kitchen cabinet.

"What now?" he asked, after he'd downed it.

"Grain Jackson and I'll find something for you to eat."

"Then what?"

"We set some traps, and with luck, will catch some skunks."

"Big traps for skunks," he said.

"Big skunks," I said, grabbing up one of the traps and leading him out.

## Chapter Nineteen

SADDLING DUSTY while Iggy ate some beans and bread, courtesy of Maddy, I made sure my pair of LeMats were loaded and in their saddle holsters, and my old Winchester fully loaded and in the saddle scabbard. Then I led him out into the brush and staked him out in some tall sage.

The barn had a hayloft, loading doors with block and tackle front and back, and a trap door leading out to the roof, which was a mite steep for moving about. Still, I swung all doors, including the trap door, wide open. From the hayloft, I had three fields of fire. I loaded the Sharps and left it in the loft with a handful of the big 45-90 cartridges at hand.

The sage and brush surrounding the house and barn on three sides was beginning to dry out as spring was done sprung, and summer coming on.

Reverend McGregor kept a hogshead of kerosene in the barn and I filled three buckets. Angel and I took them out into the brush on three sides, strategically hiding them, after I'd hidden the Yellow Boy near the hogshead along with a box of .44 shells. The brush was far back from the house and barns, so a fire started there would be little danger to the structures.

I made sure both of us had a few Lucifers to strike up and use to light up things if need be.

As dusk was about upon us, I returned to the house and revealed my plan to place the traps, and cautioned them should they need to escape the place. The traps would not know friend from enemy and I'd hate to be the cause of one of Maddy's pretty legs being left in the dirt somewhere. She agreed.

Using the three-foot-long pry bar that had come with the huge traps, I sat the first one on the trail coming in from the smoke trees, just fifty yards from my room, and the second between a pair of junipers, where a wide game trail led to one of the pasture's water troughs. As if we were trapping wary animals, I covered them with light debris and dirt and sage trash, where they couldn't be seen. I didn't bother to chain them down, as these animals would not drag them after being caught. The sage was thick on either side, and if someone wanted to approach the place unseen, that was the only place to avoid the hayloft doors and the trap door in the roof of the barn.

A half-dozen smaller traps were set at twenty foot intervals in a semi-circle around my room on the side of the barn, leaving the space between my room and the house free of impediments. The smaller traps would serve more as a warning and surprise, as they'd only snap hock high on a man and would not break bone—still, one would hate the pain and surprise.

When we were done, I had a straight talk with the boy. "Angel, you've done enough. I don't want you here when the shooting starts."

"Here, or taking my chances out in the sagebrush, Señor. I will not leave."

"Then I want you in my room, and I want you to shoot the first som'bitch who sticks his nose in the door with that old Remington of your'n. It won't be me, unless I yell out first, so you just fire away."

"I will shoot him between his eyes."

"You shoot him dead center between his useless tits, and that will do just fine."

"As you wish, Señor."

I walked to the house and rapped on the door.

"Tag?" I heard the reverend call out.

"It's me. I'm gonna hide out now. The boy's in my room, the safest place I could figure, so don't let fly that way. Now, y'all leave the lights out, as if you were not home or already under the covers, and stay low."

"Will do," he called through the window, and I headed for the hayloft.

The moon was nigh to full and only two widths over the horizon when I heard the trap on the trail slam shut and a man scream a curdling yell that would freeze your backbone.

It sent a chill down mine, but I couldn't help but smile. I strained to see into the distance, but couldn't make them out. Had the moon been higher...

I could hear men mumbling, trying, I suppose, to get the trap open. I knew those traps and what they could do. If it closed on a man's leg it would likely be almost knee high, and without the pry bar would take three men to get it open...and then the man who was hit would have a damn nigh severed leg if he didn't leave the lower part on the trail for the coyotes.

It was thirty minutes—an eternity—before there was sign of them again. I imagine they had returned to the smoke trees and got a tourniquet on the man's stub, or had someone tie him to a saddle and head for Doc Ironsmith's. If so, two would be out of the fight, if not, one for sure.

I kept moving back and forth from one end of the barn to the other, studying the terrain, watching for movement. The moon now higher, the view getting better and better. I had to laugh quietly again, as this time they were coming with torches, not lamps, but torches made of sage, making fine targets of them even in the lousy light they cast.

With their numbers, they had far too much confidence.

And they came from both directions, from the trail from the smoke trees, where they'd already lost a man, and from out of the sage.

I moved back and forth from one hay door to the other, finally settling on the ones coming in from the sage. They were following the game trail to the spot between the junipers where the second bear trap rested, and there were three of them. And I knew damn well they wouldn't see our set by the light of a burning bit of sage—hell, I'd set those traps many a time where a bear didn't see nor smell them and a man was a much easier prey.

And although I could have dropped one easily with the Sharps, at seventy-five yards or so, I wanted at least two of the three to fall. So I bided my time, and must have missed one or more of them coming from the smoke trees, as a gunshot roared from below, from my room or nearby. I moved quickly to as close as I could get to over my room, and yelled out, "Boy, you okay?"

"*Sí. Uno mas.*"

I knew enough Spanish to know that meant "one more." Getting back to my position, I could see the three now running, not knowing there were two of us, probably thinking they now knew where I was, as the shot had come from my room.

I set up with the heavy rifle resting against the jamb of the big double door. One man passed the set between the junipers, then another, and to my surprise, all three made it past safely. I zeroed on the man in the lead, and the big rifle leapt in my hands. He did a complete backward somersault. The man behind him dove for the bushes, but the third man turned and ran back the way they'd come, but only made two strides before the reverberating clang of the trap and his scream echoed across the barnyard.

Then the jambs of the doors splintered around me and I spun away, my own side erupting in blood. I crawled into the hay and felt for my wound, surprised that I was holed through and through, but only just below the rib cage and an inch or so in from my side. It had missed bone and if it hadn't caught a bowel, I'd heal. I laughed to myself, even though the pain had my eyes watering and my butt puckered, as the funny part was why did I think I'd live long enough to heal?

I gathered my wits about me, my cartridges, ran for the front of the barn, slung the rifle across my back, and latched onto a pair of the ropes in the block and tackle, leaping into the darkness. To my surprise, I hadn't grabbed opposing ropes, and went almost freely the twelve feet to the soft ground of the barnyard. There had been some resistance in the ropes, so I didn't hit as hard as I might have, but still it rocked me.

And it wasn't a bad thing, as shots cut the air over my head. Had I come down slowly…

I dove, rolled and ducked back inside the barn, plunged to the side and hunkered down behind some grain sacks, fighting for breath.

Jerking my broken saber I cut a couple of pieces of shirttail and stuffed my wound, front and back. Tears filled my eyes as the pain made me gasp, but I finally contained them, knowing I had to see to shoot.

I moved to the back of the barn again, picking up the Yellow Boy along the way and hiding the Sharps where it had been, then heard Angel. "Señor, you okay?"

"Yes," I called out, then snapped, "Shut up, boy." We had to stop this yelling back and forth as it gave away our positions. Then I heard him kicking at the board wall between barn and my room, and in a moment he had a couple of boards kicked loose, and was scrambling through.

"Whisper," I said. And he moved close to me so he could be heard.

"There must be ten or twelve, Señor," he said.

"Damned if there wasn't a bunch of shooting."

"How long can we last?"

"We got lots of shells, but they know where we are. You remember the water ditch, about twenty feet over there?" I pointed to the side of the barn, where a now unused ditch crossed the barnyard to the pasture."

"*Sí.*"

"I'm going to throw a few shots around, and I want you to run for the ditch, stay low, and dive in. Follow it until you're close to where we hid the kerosene. Throw it around the brush, light it up, and hightail it out into the sage. Don't stop. Keep running, all the way back to Henderson's. You've done enough."

A couple of shots cut the air through the barn and we hunkered lower.

"Move to the back door, stay low, and wait for me to begin pouring lead out that way, then hightail it."

"I will, but I will hunt in the brush. You are holding your side, Señor?"

"Just a scratch. Stay low, so you don't get scratched. And you head for Henderson's."

"*Sí*, Señor. When this is over."

And he moved away. Damn hardheaded kid.

Before he got in position, I heard another trap

snap, and a man curse…one of the smaller ones set outside my room.

I don't believe I'd ever had a more successful trap line, I thought, smiling I levered in a shell, and let fly a half-dozen shots out the back doors, seeing Angel slip through as I did so. Quickly I changed position, as my muzzle flashes had given me away.

A dozen shots cut the air and slammed into the barn walls, sending splinters flying.

Then I heard Maddy scream.

## Chapter Twenty

I RAN for the front of the barn, and tried to make out what was going on in the house, but could see nothing. Again, she screamed out of the darkness of the house.

Then the side of the house lit up and for a fleeting second I thought it was afire, but it was a reflection of the growing fire off to the side of the barn. Angel had done his work. Two quick gunshots rang out from that direction, and for a second I was torn—go see what I could do for Angel, should he be in trouble, or charge the house?

I didn't know that Angel had trouble, and knew from the scream that Maddy did, so my mind was made up for me, and I charged the house, shots kicking up dirt around my feet and cutting the air around us, whistles of death. I didn't pause to turn the knob, but crashed through the door, into the two big barrels of the reverend's shotgun staring me in the face.

"It's me, it's me," I yelled and he lowered the muzzle.

"Maddy screamed," I said, but I could see her, bent over Ranger, scratching his ears and talking low to him.

"That Indian of Dillon's tried to get in the front door, but Ranger met him and got a piece of his hide. The Indian hightailed it."

"So, you're okay?"

"Fine," Maddy said, then asked, "Angel?"

"Don't know, but I'm going to find out. Is there a window out of the bedrooms?"

"Both have windows," she said.

"Follow me, and close and lock it behind."

She nodded and I head into what turned out to be her room, with a window facing away from the barn and my room, where the fire had been concentrated. Hoping they'd figure me to come back out the door, I dropped out and ran for the sage, but now, in the light of the fire, I was in plain view.

Again, the ground kicked up around me and I could feel a shot slap at the back of my right leg, but I didn't slow.

When I got in the cover of the brush, I fingered the hole in my pant leg, found a burn where the slug had slithered across my thigh, but no real damage, and, still carrying the Yellow Boy and jamming shells in as I did so, ran the hundred yards to where I'd staked Dusty.

As I was unstaking and mounting him, I took count. Angel said there were ten to twelve of them, how he knew I had no idea, but I didn't doubt him. Traps had taken out two for sure, my Sharps one, and Angel's Remington one, so if only ten, I was back to that magic number of six. Damn, it seemed I just couldn't get ahead.

However, at least two of those down were the culprits who'd attacked the Bar M, and with any luck, some of the other four were among them. I just hoped I would live to find out.

The fire was growing, but moving away from the barn and house. I spurred the big horse out into the darkness, slipped the Winchester out of the scabbard and the Yellow Boy in, slung the Winchester over my back, put the reins in my teeth, and palmed the two LeMats.

I didn't think they'd expect me to be mounted, so I circled the house and rode directly toward the trail from the smoke trees. Circling in the darkness, I charged out of the backlight of the fire, and in seconds was bearing down on four men who stood talking, probably figuring their next move. They looked up, but I imagine they figured I was one of the three who'd gone to the other side of the barn, and thinking I'd rein up, but instead I gave Dusty my heels, which I seldom if ever did, and drove the big horse directly into them.

They scattered, with me firing at least six shots from both weapons as I charged through. I stopped when I again reached darkness, changed the pins over to the shotgun shells, and gave the horse my heels again. Seeing the clearing light up with their muzzle blasts, I got off one shotgun shell, seeing a man fold. Then Dusty folded under me and I pitched over his head, rolling into the sage. Even after somersaulting I ended up on my feet, LeMats still in hand, and running, shots cutting the air around me.

I dove into the sage, and moved as quickly as I could, trying not to think about my trusty old horse, crabbing until I had them between me and the distant fire. They were backlit, but seemed too stupid to realize it, and I brought the second LeMat to bear on a man who must have been thirty yards distant. The gun bucked in my hand, and the man screamed, but he spun and ran. Too far for the shotgun shell to do much.

Backing into the sage, I changed the pins back to cartridge, then settled down and waited in silence.

I could see two of the four who'd been in the group, hiding low, behind a clump of sage. I unslung the Winchester, and to my surprise found the lever severely bent. My tumble had not been uneventful.

I cast it aside and raised the LeMat in my right hand, centering it on one of the men hiding forty yards away, but before I could fire a shot rang out from my distant left and he tumbled backward out of sight. I'd caught a glimpse of the muzzle blast, and moved that way until I thought I was twenty paces from where it had come from, and called out, "Angel?"

"*Sí*," came the whispered reply.

I guess I'd yelled a little louder than I'd meant to, as firing erupted and bullets cut the air. Both of us hit the ground, and I could hear him scrambling closer, then his whisper.

"Some of them rode away." As he said that, I could hear more hoof beats from the other side of the house.

"There's at least one more near the one you shot, unless he slipped away."

"I will go back to the barn and the hay loft. Maybe I can see him from there."

"I'll give you some covering fire. Be careful."

"*Sí*." And he was gone.

I gave him the count of ten, then let fire in the direction of where the two had been hiding. But got no return fire.

So I settled back, and waited.

But didn't have to wait long. Angel's Remington barked from the hayloft and a man screamed, and I could see him running across the barnyard, if you can call dragging a leg running. I moved back to where Dusty had fallen, and to my great sadness, found him breathing erratically. I searched him over in the darkness and found he was shot both gut and chest, and blood flowed freely from his mouth and nostrils, and pink lung blood bubbled from the hole in his chest. With a catch in my throat and burning eyes, I lay muzzle to his head, and put him to sleep. It was a gunshot that would echo in my heart for as long as I lived. I was able to pull the Golden Boy from the scabbard, and found it in good working order.

Laying a hand on his neck, I said a silent prayer that the good and faithful horse he was, was now in horse heaven with cool green pastures and clean clear flowing water.

I gritted my teeth in anger and settled down in the darkness, to wait and see what transpired.

Nothing moved for two hours by the movement of the moon, so I finally rose, stretched, and walked to the barn, just as if I was out on a Sunday stroll.

I almost tripped across a man laying outside my door, but it was obvious he was to be no more trouble, so I called out to Angel as I bent to stare into the open dilated eyes of Willy Stark, the scar on his face clear in the moonlight.

And another filthy killer bites the dust.

"You okay, boy?"

"*Sí*. Are they gone?"

"No one tried to blow me in half as I came over this way, so I'd say yes, they are gone."

"Then I will come down."

"I'm going to check on the McGregor's," I said, and headed for the house.

The fire had burned itself out, stopping on the edge of a distant sandy ravine, so I had nothing to worry about there. The view from the McGregor place would stink for a while, but nature had a way of greening things up in a hurry, particularly in the high desert.

I whistled as I reached the back door, and shouted out as I entered.

Silence.

It was empty, except for my dying dog, again shot, but this time through the chest. He lasted only minutes, his head in my lap, his breath ragged until it stopped altogether.

This time the tears were not from the pain of a wound in my side, but from a deep wrenching wound in my heart.

But I didn't have time to mourn as the reverend and Maddy were nowhere to be found.

I did have time to grow insatiably angry.

And I wasn't the only one. I returned to the barnyard to find Angel urinating in Willy Stark's staring, unmoving, face.

I guess Angel was better at showing his anger than I was. He was well my junior, and I should have been the one to teach the whelp some manners, but in that instance, I couldn't bring myself to correct him.

## Chapter Twenty-One

THERE WAS no sense trying to track them in the dark, not that I would have to as I was sure the trail would lead directly to the Lazy Snake.

And I couldn't imagine they would hurt the reverend and his daughter, nonetheless...They were a lowlife bunch, so I couldn't be sure. I decided to survey the battleground then try and figure what to do. My side, still weeping blood, was getting stiff as hell, and I was having to stop and catch my breath and get the dizziness to stop...but on examining my wound in the light of McGregor's kerosene lamp, I doubted if the slug had caught bowel so I guessed I'd live, if the green rot didn't set in.

We decided to catch a little sleep in shifts, then with the morning light, so still I could barely move, we walked out and circled round the place, finding each location where we thought a body might be found, and we found five of them, but only two who I recognized. Willy Stark and Tate Jorgensen were both down from gunshots, Willy by Angel's Remington and Tate with half his chest blown away by my big Sharps.

The one I'd shot just before Angel had fired from the sage was wounded and I doubted would last the day, but he was a fella I'd never laid eyes on before, and a blood trail led from where Angel had shot the other one to where he'd managed to mount a horse and ride off.

A six foot circle of blood was around the first trap, the one on the trail leading in from the smoke-trees, and the other, near where Tate had fallen, had captured another fella I'd not laid eyes upon. He was a husky sort, big as a hogshead barrel and ugly as the hog it was named after, and he was dead from bleeding out, I guessed, as he had no other wound other than where his leg had been snapped three quarters through. He'd dragged the trap fifty paces, and left a thick trail of blood all that way.

In surveying the rest of the scene, I figured nine riders had come to pay us a visit, and only five had ridden away. Not a bad night's work for a gimpy ex-soldier and a Mexican sheepherder who was yet to reach his majority.

I was happy with it.

Four of those who'd laid my sister and her family in their graves were now in or staring into the deep darkness of theirs, and I was not a bit saddened by the fact another four had met their maker along the way. For they had been doing the devil's work, as I considered Dillon the devil on earth.

They should have picked better company.

Now it was the Indian, Crooked Arm; Seth Rheinhart, Dillon's nephew; Shank Cavanaugh, and the herb bull Colonel Mace Dillon, and my promise to myself and to my sister's ghost would be fulfilled.

By the time we harnessed the McGregor's freight/hay wagon, dragged my good horse Dusty off into the burned sage until we found a decent spot to leave him to the critters—ashes to ashes, dust to dust—loaded the four bodies on the wagon along with the wounded and comatose cowhand, and had buried my good dog, I was wondering if I was going to live to see another day.

We had no other choice, as I could not sit up to hold the traces. Angel had to drive me to find the doc so he could treat me and the comatose cowhand, even if it meant Angel might end up in the hoosegow.

I guess I passed out, almost before we were out of the barnyard, as I awoke in strange surroundings, not unpleasant, but strange and new to me, and I had a dressing on my side.

Even then, for a fleeting second, I thought maybe I was dead, as it was a beautiful woman, near an angel, bending over me.

But it wasn't a spirit, it was Lizzy, with a glass of spirits in hand.

"Howdy," I said, but so tired I could barely keep my eyes open to admire her.

"Howdy yourself. You're in my rooms, out behind Sally's. Doc said with luck you'll be fine. You lost a lot of blood."

"I'm—"

"Don't talk, rest. Nobody knows you're here but the doc, John Pointer, and Judge Thorne. Doc had to go out to the Lazy Snake, as it seems a bunch of his hands are all shot up. Doc and Mayor Pointer are telling Dillon that they put you on yesterday's train for San Francisco."

"Pity," I mumbled. "I was just gettin' to like the place."

"Yes, a real pity."

"Go to sleep. I'll have some soup for you when you wake up…then we are putting you on a train out of Nemesis."

I avoided a response to that, and instead asked, "Angel?"

"Last I heard he's in jail, in a cell with Natchez Pete and that fella you brought in."

"Damn it."

"I'll make sure he eats well. The judge is getting ready to try Natchez Pete, so the boy will have to wait a good long while before he comes before the court. He'll be fine."

Then it dawned on me. "Maddy and the reverend?"

"Out at Dillon's place, or so it's been reported. The judge rode out with the doc to see them, as you were raving about them in your stupor."

"I hope they're okay."

"No reason they shouldn't be," she said, innocently. "We'll know tomorrow."

"Bull crap. Dillon's a pig in silk shirts. His sons a bitches killed my horse and my dog...both of them far better critters than Dillon and his swine."

With that she laughed, then her tone turned serious. "I'm real sorry about your animals."

"Me too. Sleep," I mumbled, my eyelids heavy as anvils.

"Yes, sleep."

It took a week for me to regain my strength. Doc Ironsmith had told Lizzy that it was loss of blood that took me down, and, God willing, I'd be back to normal in a few days. I was unable to watch Natchez Pete get his neck stretched, but that's okay, as before this was over I'd have a dozen lifetimes of watching folks die.

The hell of it is, the judge reported that yes, Maddy and the reverend were out at Dillon's, but were on a sightseeing ride around the ranch, according to Dillon, and so the judge missed them. So no one had seen or heard of them since.

I strapped my gun back on my hip on Tuesday morning, just as Lizzy arrived with my breakfast.

"It's too soon, Tag," she said.

"Too soon for what?" I asked.

"You know damn well for what. To go back out on the street, that's what. And besides, who'll I play cribbage with?"

"Lizzy, you are a princess, and if life were my own, I'd never leave here."

She laughed. "Now, I didn't mean that much cribbage," then she turned serious again. "Don't go out, Tag."

"I've got to finish this, Lizzy, and I've got to find out what's up with Maddy and her father. It's my fault—"

"You said they insisted you stay."

"They did, but still, had I not been a tenant of theirs, none of this would have happened to them."

"So, you think you're going out to the Lazy Snake?"

"Unless you know another way."

"How about I go out there, take some of the girls? A social call. I might even make some money."

"I thought Bridgid told me, long ago, that the colonel was against sporting women in his town?"

"He is, for everyone other than the colonel."

"The hell you say."

"I say the truth. And he likes them skinny, as skinny as Bridgid."

"No."

"Yes, every Saturday afternoon for the last couple of years, that's why she had to quit socializing. She's his, exclusively. She meets him at the Mystic, four sharp, every Saturday. He often stays over in the Mystic's best rooms for church on Sunday...to come back to Jesus, I guess."

I had to laugh at that one. "And no one else knows?"

"No one else would say they knew, if they knew."

"I'm headed to my office."

"How are you going to explain a week missing?"

"Might not have to, and I have to see about Angel and get him out before he gets a year or two in the pen."

"I didn't tell you, but they gave your job to Shorty."

Now that one really made me laugh and slap my thighs. "The hell you say. He couldn't spit in a bucket if his head was in it."

She was silent for a long moment, then for the first time, reached up and put her arms around my neck. "I'm getting attached to you, Tag. I don't want to be puttin' flowers on your headstone."

"Hell, I couldn't afford a headstone, Lizzy. I imagine they'll just leave me out in the desert for the coyotes, like I had to leave ol' Dusty."

"You got any feelings for me, Tag?"

It was my turn to get serious. "Lizzy, I got a job of work to do, and I'm surprised I've lived this long. Should I finish it, and finish it in one piece, which I doubt, I'd like to talk on that some more."

I gave her a chaste kiss on the cheek, and pulled away.

"Don't go, Tag. I'll sell this place and we can go to Nevada City, or San Francisco, and start up another saloon. You can sit shotgun, and I'll run the place. You owe me a bunch of baths, and you can pay them back...and more."

I was a little taken aback at this beautiful woman's straight talk. She'd been caring for me for a week, giving me baths with a wet rag—not in personal places, but more personal than any woman ever had—and been feeding me until I could climb in a tub on my own power and feed myself. And, come to think of it, I was damn pleased with the whole arrangement, and didn't want to walk back out on a Nemesis street and face whoever was left of the Lazy Snake riders.

It was a tempting proposition, and had I not made a promise to myself and to my sister's ghost....

"I got to go, Lizzy. I'll be back, God willin' and the creek don't rise."

She sighed deeply. "What kind of flowers did you say you wanted?"

"Lizzy belles, prettiest flower in the whole world," I said, with a smile, and turned and walked out. Wentworth's horse was tied outside the office, alongside Shorty's.

"What the hell," Wentworth said when I walked in. He stared at me for a long moment. Shorty stood slack jawed, then finally sputtered, "I think...I thought...I was told...you're supposed to be in San Francisco."

"Nope. Congratulations, I'm told you're the new City Marshal."

He stiffened. "Yep, and I'm keeping the job."

"You're welcome to it, Shorty."

I turned to Wentworth. "And congratulations to you, sheriff. I hear you brought Natchez Pete back in and earned that fat reward."

"I did, and I'm keepin' it."

"And you're welcome to it."

"You got some answering to do?"

"Regarding?"

"A wagon load of dead bodies."

"In the line of duty, sheriff. Remember, I was the

city marshal, and I was attacked by a platoon of assholes."

"Humph," he said.

"You want a statement, I'll run the judge down and bring him over and he can sit in—"

"Judge left town, right after the trial."

"How about the kid?"

"What kid?" he asked, which surprised me a little.

"Angel Sanchez, who I heard was in your jail."

"So now it's my jail."

"He was in the goddamn jail. You know exactly who I'm talking about."

"Oh, that kid. We let him go. He's back out at Henderson's."

"Oh, yeah. I'll ride out and say hello."

"He's not there, said he was going back to Mexico."

"Bullshit, Wentworth."

He shrugged, and gave me a smug look. "That's what he tol' me, he was going straight back which was one of the reasons I let him out."

I stared at him until he cut his eyes away, and I knew he was lying. If he'd hurt that kid, his name went on my list.

The damned list just don't ever seem to go down.

"Colonel Dillon wants to have a confab with you, Slade," Wentworth said.

I stretched and yawned, and replied, "I was thinking about taking a ride out that way."

"Maybe I'll ride along with you. I'd enjoy seeing the Lazy Snake boys take you down."

"Bet you would. I got some things to do here in town first."

"Right. Hear you lost that big ugly dog, and your horse."

"Yep. I heard Dillon lost that bull he prizes so much."

Wentworth looked puzzled. "I didn't hear that."

"Well, you're not a soothsayer, and I just might be." I moved to the door, left without a goodbye or go to hell, and headed for Sally's.

Tobin "Curly" Stewart, Dillon's range boss, was at the bar, alone, having breakfast. He looked up as I entered and casually laid a palm on the butt of his sidearm.

## Chapter Twenty-Two

I HADN'T TRADED two words with the man since I'd been in town, as unlike the rest of the Lazy Snake riders, he seemed to mind his own business. But maybe now was the time to get to know the gent. I saddled up near the bar stool next to him, just like I was somebody.

He looked me up and down, then asked straight out, "You got a bone to pick with me?"

"You tell me. If I do, I don't know about it."

He nodded and seemed to relax, then confidently gave me his back and went back to his breakfast.

When I climbed up on the stool next to him, he again eyed me carefully. "I thought you was in California?"

"Oh, is that the word out at the Lazy Snake?"

"It was. But the boss man out there didn't believe it. He thinks you been hiding out somewheres."

"He does, does he?" I said.

"He did anyway. I'm no longer employed there, so I don't know what he's thinking today."

"You quit?"

"Let's just say, I'm no longer employed out there."

Polkinghorn wiped the bar coming our way, looking a little concerned. "You eating or drinking or both?" he asked.

"I'll have some eggs and a slab of meat."

"And coffee?"

"Why not. And some toasted bread and some of that good yellow jam."

Bridgid Fimple came in from the kitchen about that time, carrying that big enameled coffee pot. She stopped and her eyes flared, seeing me. I guess Lizzy had not told even ol' skinny Bridgid that I was under her wing, but then knowing she was tight with Dillon, I understood why.

"Another cup, and tell cookie another breakfast," Polkinghorn yelled at her across the saloon, and she spun and quickly came back in carrying another cup as well.

"So," I said to Stewart, "you headed out of town? Not much call for a ranch foreman anywhere else here abouts."

"I am. If the next train has a livery car to take my horse and rig, I'm headed west."

"If you don't mind my asking, what came down between you and Dillon?"

He didn't speak for a long moment, carefully chewing his breakfast, sipping some coffee, then turned to me. "I do mind your asking, to be truthful, but I'm going to tell you anyway. He's got Miss Maddy McGregor there and her father. He's not exactly kidnapped them, keeping them in high style, but making lots of excuses as to why they can't return to town, to the point of obstinate. I don't abide by a man mistreating a woman, and told him so. He, needless to say, disagreed, and for that and other disagreements, he gave me the boot."

"For what purpose is he holding her?"

"I think, he thinks you're still in the neighborhood. He made some inquiries with the doc and with the ticket agent at the train station, and he's not convinced that he's getting the truth about you being gone. Ticket agent said you boarded no train that he knew of. I think Dillon's hoping you'll show up out his way. He's got his hackles up over you...to say the least."

"The hell you say," I chuckled at that.

"I say."

"I'd hate to disappoint the colonel," I said, giving his former *segundo* a tight smile.

"Take an army," Stewart said.

"Where's that new bull he crows about?"

"Why?"

"Just wondered.  Figured he built him a palace, the way he goes on about him."

"Fact is he built him his own little barn, out past the big barn, with his own paddock and water and such.  He's a fine looking animal, but you'd think he was Dillon's own flesh and blood, the way he goes on about him."

"Naw, he's way prettier than Dillon, I'd guess."

Steward laughed at that.

Bridgid Fimple arrived with my breakfast, and it was a while before we talked anymore.

He wiped his mouth and stood, dropping a fifty cent piece on the bar.

"You headed back out to the Snake?" I asked.

"Never again.  But he'll know you're about before morning's out," he said, eyeing Bridgid Fimple across the room.

"Good, maybe he'll send some more boys in to call on me."

Curly Stewart laughed with that.  "Doubt it.  He's got a man with a new peg leg being fitted, and are already short some other hands as I hear you know well.  I imagine he'll wait for you to come calling."

"Ain't he the clever one," I said.

"He is that, Slade. Put some holes in his silk shirt for me, you get the chance." He tipped his hat, and walked out.

"Good luck, Curly," I called after him, and he waved over his shoulder.

Polkinghorn came back to where I sat and collected the four bits off the bar.

"You have any idea what they did with the boy, Angel Sanchez?" I asked the tall barman.

"The judge cut him loose," he said.

"The hell you say."

"I say. The judge sent him packing before he left town. I imagine the boy was headed back to Roland Henderson's place. Wentworth and Dillon was mad as hell about it."

I sighed deeply, relieved that the boy was okay. "Anybody been watching the McGregor's place since they've been gone?"

"Pointer's had a boy going out there to feed and water the stock."

I paid up, tipped my hat, and headed for the livery. Phinias still had the McGregor's wagon and team, and helped me harness up. Stopping at Pointer's store, I collected a number of items Lizzy told me he'd been holding for me, including my traps, my Sharps, my Winchester, and my two LeMat revolvers. My Army Colt and my stubby saber were on my belt when I was delivered to the docs, so I was pretty well whole again. Pointer informed me the gray was in the pasture at McGregor's, and Angel had left my tack in the barn.

By afternoon I was saddled on a good strong steel gray dappled gelding, had a pack animal behind me, and was on the trail. Had I half a brain, it would be on the trail back to the Salmon River country, but I've never been accused of being mentally endowed.

If Dillon suspected I'd be coming, he'd be looking for me to come from town, riding north to his main gates, so I figured to make a wide circle around the ranch and come at him from the north, and in the dead of night. In order to get anywhere near the big ol' main house, I figured I'd need a distraction, and it seemed nothing would get Dillon's attention like some trouble with that fancy new bull. Thanks to Curly Stewart, I knew just where to find him.

That bull was high priced and highly prized, but no more than I valued Ranger and Dusty. If I had my way, Dillon would die for my sister and her family, and worse, die slow for my animals, which had been my close family for a goodly long time. I had a mind to turn a fine bull backstrap over a slow fire.

Liam Toole had died at my hand in Sally's. Enrico Zaragosa from my lucky shot during the first gunfight at the McGregor's. Willy Stark had died charging into my room and into Angel's accurate

Remington during the second gun battle at McGregor's. Tate Jorgenson had half his chest blown away from the big slug of my 45-90 at about the same time.

I figured it was the Indian, Crooked Arm; Shank Cavanaugh, the gunfighter; Dillon's nephew Seth Rheinhart; and Dillon himself, then my work was done. It turned out there was nine of them who'd raided the Bar M, more than I'd figured on, but I was fifty percent home, downhill the rest of the way.

Only able to describe the time since I left the Salmon country as a rampage, I thought of the others. The two bandits who'd accompanied Natchez Pete Pelletier who I'd left in the dirt after they'd robbed Dillon's bank—hell, had I known it was Dillon's money, I'd have shot high. Pelletier himself, at the end of Judge Thorne's rope. The big man who'd died from loss of blood after getting his leg snapped off out in the sage near McGregor's. And another fella now walking with a peg leg, could I believe Curly Stewart, and I had no reason not to.

Willy Stark had fallen to Angel's shot from inside the cabin, then another had fallen to his Remington from his position in the hayloft, and another man had run from the same place, if you can call dragging a leg running.

It had been a trail of blood so far, including more

than a dollop of mine, and it wasn't over. Seven men dead and at least one crippled.

But it was my intention to make it end, and to set Maddy McGregor and the reverend on their way home.

It was clouding up, scattered, but I hoped they would gather as the moon had been bright, and light would be my enemy.

When I got to the low hills a bit over a mile north of the Lazy Snake headquarters I could see a creek bed, cut a dozen feet deep into the sage-covered flat that ran to within a quarter mile of Dillon's house, and quickly decided that would be my path, but it was still midafternoon. I made camp, rolled my bear coat out in the shade of some tall sage near the cut of the same trickle that ran past Dillon's headquarters a mile or more away, and went to sleep. I was still not back to normal, not to my full strength, and prayed I was up to the task at hand.

When I awoke, it was full dark with a fat full moon overhead. The clouds were still sparse, but I hoped getting heavier. There was a whiff of rain in the air, and it could be my friend if it came and darkened the sky. I'd slept longer than I meant to. It must have been well past midnight.

I made a pan full of soup from a handful of jerked venison and sipped it along with gnawing some hard bread I'd found in Maddy's kitchen, then saddled up, leaving the pack horse staked out in a grassy flat near the trickle of water.

With my Golden Boy fully loaded, my LeMats the same and in their saddle holsters, my Army Colts and saber on my belt, and my two shot gambler's gun in my coat pocket, I let the gray begin to pick his way down the creek bed.

It was dark as a foot up a bull's butt when I managed to spot a much smaller barn and paddock beyond the main barn. It was, I was sure, his majesty Napoleon's palace...but it wouldn't be for long.

I tied the gray to one of the river willows lining the creek and, carrying the Yellow Boy with my Army .44 in its holster, the belly gun in my coat pocket, and one of the LeMats in my belt, crept up to the edge of the embankment so I was just eye high over the rim.

It was a hundred and fifty yards or so to the building in the moonlight, and I'd be surprised if Dillon didn't have guards posted, so I hunkered down in a copse of river willows and watched...and sure enough, I saw the flare of a Lucifer near the front door on the wide porch surrounding the main house. There was most likely a man out back as well, but I doubted if there'd be a man in Napoleon's barn. I stationed myself with the barn between me and the porch and strolled over as if I owned the place.

I was wrong.

I saw the flickering light of a lamp between the barn boards, found a knothole, and took a gander, just as the notes of a flute floated my way.

In moments, I'd located the hooligan, hunkered down in a pile of loose hay, a pipe smoking near at hand, and a carved flute in his mouth. Crooked Arm wasn't bad with the instrument, and had I time I'd have sat back to enjoy his last melody. Glad that it wasn't another Lazy Snake hand I'd have to dispatch, not one of those I hunted, I flattened my back to the wall and slipped around to the front door, wondering if maybe I'd just charge in and get the drop on him, or make some noise so he'd wander out to see what was up.

The problem was, the pass-through door built into one of the barn's two wide main doors was in plain sight of the man on the porch, another hundred yards away. The good news was there was two foot of moon shadow on that side of the barn, and I was in it.

I didn't have long to contemplate, for a shepherd cow dog made up my mind.

He was only a half-dozen paces from me, and cut loose like he was part wolf, racking my backbone, tightening my butt, and straightening me so I jerked back against the barn door, making a racket that would wake a hibernating bear, much less a flute playing Shoshone.

The hound didn't fly at me but was raising hell as if he'd treed a cougar.

I pinned myself to the door, behind where the pass through would open, and waited.

In seconds, the door swung open, and I heard "Hush, dog."

## Chapter Twenty-Three

STEPPING out just far enough to do so, I brought the heavy barrel of the Yellow Boy across the Indian's pate, but it was a glancing blow and he staggered back inside. By the time I got to him he had knife in hand. I was prepared to give him the butt of the rifle to his forehead, but the blade changed my mind, and I reversed things and again swung the heavy barrel, cracking his wrist and sending the knife flying. He tried to make it past me to the door, but I kicked his legs out from under him and he went down, paining my own so much I damn near went down. Aiming at his head again, but with him scrambling, the barrel took him across the back shoulder high. He grunted and I heard his breath escape, and I was able to swing again, this time whacking him a good one across the back of the neck, and he went down like the sack of pig dung he was.

I quickly reversed the rifle and drove the butt into the back of his head, and he stilled. I doubted if he'd ever awaken as his head was well smashed.

Only then could I check my surroundings in the dim light of the kerosene lamp. The barn was only ten paces by forty. One side of the front of the barn was a grain bin, the other an enclosure for loose hay. The rear of the barn, most of the building, was a paddock for the bull, who was watching me with disdain.

Then I heard footfalls, and moved to the front of the building near the door. "What the hell are you up to?" I heard called out. As quickly as I arrived, the door swung open and a cowhand stumbled in, a badly rolled cigarette hanging from his lips. I didn't know this one.

His sidearm was still holstered, which was his mistake.

I shoved the muzzle of the rifle under his chin, and gave him some advice I figured would keep him quiet. "One little squeak out of you and the top of your head will be back in Nemesis."

His eyes flared and he carefully raised his hands. "Who are you?" I demanded.

"Hell's fire, I work here, who are you?"

"I didn't come here to palaver. I asked your name?"

"Sam. Samuel Prichard. I work here."

"Well, Sam Prichard, I can shoot a hole in you that bull could walk through, or I could tie you up. Your preference."

"Hell, no choice there. Tie me up."

There was a lead rope with a snap on the end for the bull's nose ring, so I suggested he fetch it, which he did, but he spun and tried to lash me with the heavy snap. I brought the butt of the Golden Boy up and caught him under the chin. He went down, but managed to kick me a hell of a lick on my bad knee on the way.

I crumpled, and we were both on the ground, him grabbing for his side arm, me swinging the heavy barrel, which caught him at the base of the neck. He gasped for breath, and the second swing took him across the side of the head.

He was a lot easier to handle unconscious. I was tired of killing fellows I didn't know or didn't have a grudge against, so I jerked him to his feet, walked him out the front door, where the shepherd took up his yapping again, and the cowhand stumbling like a Saturday night drunk toward the creek until I was fifty yards from the barn. His stumbling and my dragging a leg that was shooting pain all the way to the top of my head made for a tough trip. Luckily, he was wearing a dust storm sized neckerchief so I hog tied and gagged him before he came fully conscious.

Now, for the barn and the bull.

To my great surprise the Indian was stirring when I came back in, so I gave him a good whack again. He should have thanked me for it, as he was staying with the barn, a fitting end for what he did to my sister and her beautiful family, and unconsciousness would be his friend when a fire licked at his hams.

But the bull wasn't at fault. Still, should he have to go, that was just Dillon's tough luck. Much as I knew his demise would pain Dillon, I didn't plan on Dillon being around to be pained. I opened the outside gate to his corral and the doors from his paddock to the outside, then scrambled for the fence as the thought of being stomped by Dillon's bull before finishing with Dillon was not high on my list. The bull, however, didn't bother to come through the doors. I imagined he soon would, as I've never known one of God's creatures who'd run into a fire.

The kerosene lamp was still flickering, and I emptied half of its bottom well on the hay, opened the chimney, and gave it a toss. Before I could make it out the door, the hay had a good lick of fire going.

I headed straight for the house and made the front porch before the barn really lit up. The bull was smart enough to find the doors, the corral, and the open gate. By the time the flames licked through the split shingle roof, he was trotting for the high country.

Dillon's front door wasn't locked, so I walked in, limped into his parlor, and poured myself three fingers of his good whiskey, which dulled my own throbbing pains.

A full minute hadn't passed before I heard men yelling outside, and a man crashed through the front door and took the stairs three at a time, yelling for his boss man.

It wasn't another half minute before Dillon, barefoot and in nightshirt, and his man flew past the doorway to the parlor and charged outside. I walked to the window and watched them in the growing firelight hot-footing it across the barnyard. Men had poured out of the bunkhouse and taken up a water wagon and buckets. But the barn was well past that solution.

I slugged down my whiskey, slipped out of the parlor, and limped up the stairs. There were six doors off the upstairs hallway, with a window at either end of the hall. One of the doors was standing open. I peered in and figured, by the size of the room, big four poster bed, desk, table and chairs, it housed the master of the abode...who'd vacated in a hurry.

The door next to Dillon's opened before I could rap on it with the barrel of the rifle, and Maddy McGregor stood wide-eyed, a wrap around her nightgown.

"Sorry to disturb and to catch you in your bed clothes—"

"Tag. Tag Slade, what are you doing here?"

"Coming to fetch you home, and other business."

"Did you start that fire?"

"Look, Maddy, I don't have a lot of time. Do you want to get home or not?"

"Mace said he had nothing to do with that fire at the Bar M."

"Mace said?" I had to shake my head, astounded.

"Yes, he had nothing to do—"

"You're telling me you don't want to leave."

"Mace and I..."

"Then you'll pardon me, Miss McGregor," I started away.

"Tag, you'll never get away from here."

"Got here just fine, thank you, and will get away just fine."

"I doubt that."

"But you don't doubt Dillon's word."

"Mace Dillon is a Christian man, and a gentleman."

"He brought you here against your will."

"His men brought me here—"

"And Dillon wouldn't let you leave."

"He made me stay and listen, and I'm glad I did as I believe him. He's going to build papa another church—"

I laughed. "Render to Caesar the things that are Caesar's, and to God, the things that are God's."

"What does that mean?"

"It means you've done sold your soul."

She slammed the door, and I kicked it open. "Get your father and get out of this house, Maddy. It's going up just like the barn." She slammed it shut again but it bounced open as I had damaged it badly. And as I headed for the stairway, I heard her shouting out her window, "Mace! Mace! Help, he's in here."

I paused in the kitchen, where Chang was lighting a lantern, thinking I'd take it from him and use it to flame the house, but I couldn't bring myself to do so with Maddy and her father upstairs. I'd become a stone cold killer, but I couldn't take the risk of burning alive two who'd helped me at one time, no matter how astray they'd drifted.

I've been wrong about many things in my life, but never quite as mistaken as I was about Maddy McGregor. I'd never have guessed her one to bow under the weight of gold.

So I charged out the back door and headed for the brush, in the opposite direction as where the gray was tied. It would be a long circle to take to get back to my horse with my leg paining me but that I had to do.

The hell of it was, I'd planned to end this all this night, and had only accomplished one more body, that of Crooked Arm who I was sure was now cooked meat.

Still I had three to go. Cavanaugh, Dillon, and his nephew, Rheinhart.

Then I saw Shank Cavanaugh, tying his saddled mount up to the rail in front of a smaller house out behind the bunkhouse.

My backbone flashed a lightning bolt as hot as the barn, which was now falling in on itself, and I headed at a limping but determined stride toward the gunfighter. Two dozen men stood far enough back from the barn to escape being scorched, hands on hips, watching, transfixed, I hoped, as if they turned, I'd be in easy rifle shot range…but they held buckets, not rifles.

My Golden Boy was cocked and in hand, so no matter how Cavanaugh might have healed up from my beatings, I had the advantage.

From fifty yards away, the burning barn almost two hundred yards the other way, I shouted. "Cavanaugh!" He didn't hear me, finished tying the horse, and was moving to loosen the animal's latigo, when I shouted again from forty yards.

"Cavanaugh!"

He glanced up, put a hand up to his ear, signaling that he couldn't hear, and started my way. Obviously, he had yet to recognize me, but when I stopped at thirty-five yards and brought the rifle to my shoulder, a long pistol shot but nothing for the Golden Boy, he stopped short, and stared.

Then he slapped leather.

Even as ready as I was, he got off the first shot, which cut the air near my head. My shot spun him, and he went down, but up on one elbow, still firing.

I felt burning lead slap my thigh, levered in another shell and snapped off a shot, and this one knocked him to flat on his back. Stumbling forward, levering in another shell, I fired again, and his body jerked then shuddered. By the time I reached him, he was still, his eyes wide open. I felt a shot of remorse...not for him, but for the fact I wanted him to die slow and hard, damn the luck.

Hearing running men approaching and shouting, I wasted no time raising my remaining good leg into the stirrup. It was all I could do to get into the saddle, but I managed and bent low as lead cut the air all around me. I gave a heel to the horse, and he responded with a leap and was gaining strides until we disappeared into the brush.

At a pounding gallop, I circled back to where the gray was tied. I was able to get his reins tied to his saddle horn and pounded away. He was a good animal, and followed. I knew I was in for the ride of my life, as all of those obliged to the Lazy Snake were fine horsemen and rode for the brand.

They'd be hot on my trail, and if they got close enough, the lead would be flying.

The hell of it is, I'm bleeding again, and I can't imagine I've got a lot to spare. Slowing enough I jerk my pants belt off and get it tight around my upper thigh, north of the wound, pulling it as tight as I can stand.

I had to find a place to hole up, at least long enough to get the bleeding from my thigh stopped, before I died in the saddle.

## Chapter Twenty-Four

I FIGURED they wouldn't follow until light, three hours or so away, so I had some time to put some distance between us. So long as I stayed conscious. Staying in the little creek bottom I was able to hide my trail for a while, but it wouldn't fool a tracker as even the slow-moving creek would show tracks. A mile or so from where I'd tied the gray, we pulled up out of the crick into heavy sage, then up again onto a granite outcropping. I had high hopes it would not be marked by the horses, but as both of them were shod, I wasn't confident. To a real hand, iron shoes would mark granite just as well as soft ground.

There was some benefit coming, with God's help. The moon was only occasionally peeking through the growing cloud cover, and more and more my smeller said rain marching our way.

Another half mile and I was into cedars, sparse at first, then thick as flies on a fresh road apple. I had to take up the gray's lead rope, which was more than occasionally hard on the thigh, dragging him our way in the thick cover.

Every hundred yards I'd make a ninety degree turn, but always climbing, until I noticed the occasional pine, then no cedars and we were into a pine forest.

The distant flash of lightning, then on the count of only two, a deep rolling grumble of thunder. Only two miles away I hoped, and even more so hoped it was heading my way. A good gully washer would be the good Lord's blessing, as it would wash my tracks away, both in the creek and in the cedars.

And it was time, as each time I had to reach back to jerk the gray on, I was getting dizzy. I figured I had best find a place to hole up, somewhere I could occasionally take a gander at my backtrail.

The old man in the heavens kept answering me, as I came upon a vertical cliff, and soon a crack in it led me into a fissure. It wasn't a cave, and only ten or so feet across the bottom, but it had walls a hundred feet high, and kept most of the rain out. I had no idea where it led, or how deep the cut went into the Cliffside, but it was shelter of a sort and rose high enough over the plain to be able to see my backtrail.

I staked the horses out, but only loosened their latigos, leaving the saddles in place; finding a slight indentation in the wall, I rolled up in my bear coat. I dare not start a fire, and it might just be days before I risked one, if I lasted days. Checking the wound in my thigh as best I could, I found it weeping, but only slightly. It, at least, was through and through and had shed the lead and not hit bone. In seconds, the past was just that, the past, and my now was deep and dark, if tumultuous.

For a change I didn't dream of my sister and her family, but almost as bad, of Dusty and Ranger. I don't know if it was the flash of lightning or the almost continuous rumble and crack of thunder, but it was not an easy sleep...it was all gunfire, flashing blades, and blood and crying men and animals. And I awoke in a sweat.

But I had made it to light, and midmorning if the shadows of the pines were an indication. I'd slept far longer than I would have thought I would, but didn't feel rested. There was something about the rain that was sleep-inducing even with the dreams, and it was coming steadily. The trickle that had been a foot wide was now three feet and growing.

And there's something about having a dozen or more riders dogging your trail that interferes with your rest, and I was sure that was the case.

There was still a handful of jerky in my saddlebag, but no bread since I'd curled up in the night. The widening trickle in the bottom of the fissure made me believe the cut might go deeper into the cliff side than just a split in the cliff—the water had to be coming from somewhere. Now that it was light, I could see a hundred yards or more back into the cut. It seemed to widen.

I suddenly discovered I'd be investigating just how deep it went, for I heard men shouting and the neighing of a horse. It sure as hell didn't seem I'd be going back the way I'd come in. I've known these high desert canyons before, and rain can mean merely a greening of the countryside, or a rampaging wall of water that can roil and roll you and your horse to a watery demise. I could be riding away from death, but I could also be riding into it.

Moving as quickly as my thigh and still healing side and shot up thigh would allow, I rolled my coat and tied it behind the gray's saddle, sucked up the cinches on both of them, and this time mounted the gray and led Cavanaugh's horse, which in the light turned out to be a handsome colored sorrel. I was a horse thief, but at least it was a handsome animal I'd pilfered.

I wished I had time to drag my trail, as there was a sand bottom in the cut, but no time. The growing water might be a sweet savior or a death angel.

Trying to make as little noise as possible, I gigged

the horses forward and we picked our way deeper, away from the opening.

Gradually, the cut widened, then narrowed again, then became a slot canyon with only a sliver of light from above, then suddenly I was confronted with a pool, looking deep, with vertical walls on the canyon sides, but with a gentle slope leading up and out the far side. Swimming the horses fifty or sixty feet would be no problem, so I gave the gray my heels and he readily plunged in, but the sorrel pulled up, jerking me out of the saddle.

Cursing, now soaking wet, I moved around behind him and gave him the boot, and he leapt halfway across the damn pool and out of my reach, so I had to swim for it. I'd hoped his tail would act as a drag rope, but it was not to be.

The hell of it was, when I reached the other side where the horses were contentedly grazing where the sun on a different day must have reached the floor of the cut, my thigh was bleeding again. I guess the water had loosened whatever scab had formed. I had to pull my belt and apply the squeeze to it again.

The depth of the water was increasing with the storm and the flow getting stronger, hock-deep across the wider canyon. I smiled, knowing that in the narrow entrance it would be knee deep or more, flowing in a roar, and that would discourage any pursuers as well as wipe out my tracks—so long as it didn't grow and wipe me out as well.

Gradually, the canyon pulled up and the walls became lower and lower until it finally opened, but steeply, into a rock and river willow-scattered clearing. Rivulets, in a fan shape, gathered to cut the slot canyon below. Far below, through the now easing rain, I could see the copse of pines at or near the canyon's opening. I listened for a long while, hoping against hope that I'd hear exactly what I heard...the sweet sound of nothing but the flow of water. Miles away, the lightning still flashed, but only the tickle of thunder reached us.

It was early afternoon, the rain had stopped, but still I was through for the day. I was soon in another thicket of pines, this time higher, and found them to be lodge poles, and I stumbled into a thicket of blow-down that made a natural corral for the horses so long as I closed one opening with a lead rope. The crazy stack of logs provided lots of dry firewood and its smoke would quickly be lost in the moist air. It was more than fair shelter for me. I took a chance and made a small fire from some very dry wood, and made another soup from the jerky, a pinch of salt scraped from the bottom of my saddle bags after a long ago broken sack, and a handful of watercress I found along a trickle of water. Then hobbled the horses as double insurance, and slept.

I awoke to a dawn sky, mottled gray and gold, to my thigh wound sealed nicely with scab, and to my horses still grazing contentedly under the lodge pole pine. It was still wet enough so my smoke would be almost undetectable, so I built up a roaring fire, dried my gear, warmed up. I needed what blood I had left to flow freely and get me healed up, and warmth seemed to help that process. For a man on the run, I was a leisurely sort. I didn't want the Lazy Snake hands to catch up with me as I still had a job of work to do...Colonel Mace Dillon, the head of the snake, and his nephew, Seth Rheinhart. To be truthful, I'd been awash in blood, and I was sick at heart with it...but a promise is a promise, even if made to a ghost.

I didn't want to kill anyone else, particularly not a man merely doing his job, riding for the brand.

And I sure as hell didn't want to get caught, as I no longer had the protection of my marshal's badge. In the eyes of Wentworth, and most of the world, I was sure I was now no more than a killer and a horse thief, and that would please him to no end.

It took me three days, taking my time, riding slowly, killing one snowshoe rabbit and roasting him, and another cotton tail when I got lower and near the Transcontinental. Then, tired, but faith somewhat renewed, I reached the high meadow where I'd found Angel. Neither he nor his brother were near, and the sheep had long ago grazed away, but the cabin was there, and some vittles were nicely stored so I could make some biscuits and fry up a little moldy but still nourishing hog belly for chewing and sopping. A tender loin of beef never tasted better. I rested for another day and a night, then followed the track and scat of the herd of woolies, until I came upon them on a grassy slope below a line of pines.

A pair of shepherds saw me from more than a quarter mile away, and I could see one of them fade up into the pines. Angel was taking no chances, I presumed, and I turned out to be right as Iggy went running for him when he recognized me.

The first thing Angel said to me was of little surprise. "You see the poster, Señor?"

"Nope."

"You are a five hundred dollar *hombre*."

"A wanted poster?" I asked.

"It was not an advertisement for your good looks," Angel said, then laughed.

"Nope," I replied. "That would be for a nickel. What am I wanted for?"

"You are a murderer and a horse thief...and they want you, or merely your head."

"Ain't that something."

"Sheriff Wentworth was here yesterday, with a posse. With God's grace, we saw their dust in the distance, and I was deep in the woods when they came."

"Good. Were they looking for you as well?"

"No mention, so perhaps no one knew I was at the McGregor's with you."

"Only the McGregor's, and deep down they're decent folks, but just saying they'll talk too much, you and Iggy should head out, soon as you can. I will rest up, heal up, then go and finish my job. You and your brother head south."

"No, Señor, I will go with you."

"You've done enough, Angel. You have avenged your father, and I have finished it for you. Cavanaugh is a dead man...I stared into his dead eyes myself."

"I hope he died hard. Where will they bury him? I will piss on his grave, in honor of my father."

"He'll be in the Lazy Snake graveyard, I'm sure. And you go pissin' around there and you'll be buried beside Cavanaugh...or fed to the coyotes. I need to rest, and you need to forget revenge. You've got yours."

He looked quizzically; then as if he heard me, but was far from satisfied.

They had a camp; canvas pack covers strung between the trees to ward off the rain and sun, a good fire pit with a pot hanger and a fine cast iron Dutch oven, a windbreak of lodge pole pine blow down...so I rolled up there and slept for most of two days. The boys were both fine hands with tortillas and they kept a pot of frijoles and meat—rabbit, rattlesnake, grouse—going at all times.

Then it came to me. "Angel, do you know what day it is?"

"*Es viernes.*"

"Sorry, English please."

"Is Friday, Señor."

I smiled, for I knew where Colonel Mace Dillon was likely to be on the morrow...and it was not on the Lazy Snake.

Even though I'd slept for two days, I ate a hardy supper of tortillas, beans, and a treat, as a lamb had been lamed and injured in a fall and the boys butchered it. Then I slept the sleep of the innocent.

Now, to get into Nemesis without being seen.

## Chapter Twenty-Five

THERE WAS ONLY one place I thought I might be welcome in Nemesis, and that was at the home of Lizzy Perlmutter, the owner of Sally's. Her house, a two-story clapboard affair with some attempt in the desert climate to make it appear as if it was in New England, rose out of a circle of green grass fifty paces behind the saloon. A couple of elm trees were already six inches in diameter, and a few planters were showing off drying primroses, daisies, and some rose bushes in bud.

The moon was occluded by clouds and it was dark as the inside of a nailed coffin.

It was four A.M. when I arrived at her place, taking the risk of putting the gray into a vacant loafing shed and corral behind the house, where I also hid one of my lever actions and the pair of

LeMats. No lights shown and I was about to try and jimmy the door, when a door slammed behind me and a lantern bobbed its way toward the house.

I jumped over the porch rail, landed quietly and having to bury the outcry I wanted to make because of the shooting pain in thigh and side, and hid behind the side of the house until I could make out Lizzy's pretty face over the lantern as she mounted the stairs. Luckily, she was alone.

"Lizzy, you should keep company until you're safe in your house."

"Damn," she said, startled, and holding the lantern out to illuminate my face over the porch rail. "Why, if it isn't the judge, jury, and executioner. I heard you walked right into the Lazy Snake and redecorated as if you owned the place."

"Word travels fast. Can I hang out with you for a while? I'd go inside and give you some busi—"

"No thanks," she said, as she quickly turned down the wick on the lantern. "You've killed half my customers already, and the other half are staying inside their houses, under their covers, until this little war of yours is *fini...c'est fini.*"

"No, you mean no thanks to my going inside Sally's, or my hanging out with you for a while?"

"Get inside," she said, and I vaulted the rail, then winced and damn near passed out from the pain. I gathered my wits and waited while she fumbled with a skeleton key and got us inside.

"You want a drink?"

"Got a lot of work to do tomorrow…I guess I mean today…but I could have a touch."

"Saturday," she said as she headed to a cabinet and pulled out a bottle and a pair of glasses. "So, it's time for all the Lazy Snake boys to arrive to hoo'ra the town. You don't figure on shootin' up my place again?"

"No, ma'am. I figure on taking it elsewhere."

"Good. You gonna get some sleep first?"

"I expect, after I kill this drink, and maybe one more if you can spare it. I've been riding over twenty miles getting here."

"And you didn't come onto Wentworth. He and a half-dozen highbinders to whom he's promised a smidgen of the reward Dillon is offering are working the hills over trying to turn you up, and I imagine turn you into worm food."

"Nope, didn't see the old boy."

"And I hope you don't," she said, and we clinked glasses and downed the three fingers of good whiskey in a gulp. She poured us another.

"Aren't you about finished with this blood trail you're following?"

"About."

We'd finished the drinks, and she wasted no time

pouring another.

She sighed deeply after downing half of that, and edged closer until she was a palm's width away and looking up into my eyes, her breasts barely brushing the front of my shirt, then her voice lowered an octave and her eyes turned liquid. I could barely hear her low whisper, but was damn glad I could.

"Tag, I'm guessing I may never see you again, so how would you like to come upstairs and...and accept my...my female hospitality before you go out into another storm of gunfire."

"Well, ma'am, I'm shot all to hell, and smell like the horse I've been on for a good long while, but if you'd accept me in that sorry state, I'd be more than honored."

"And I've not kept company with a man since I've been in Nemesis, so if that lack of practice doesn't bother you...."

"Again, I'm honored."

With that, she and I both finished the rest of our whiskey, then she reached out and took my hand, and led me up the stairs.

It was a damn good thing my business with Colonel Dillon would not commence until the afternoon, as I slept later than I had in a decade, and was called upon to accept some more female hospitality after I awoke, well after the sun was over the yardarm. My leg and my side pained me something terrible, but I was not surprised that I oft times forgot I had a side and a thigh.

I can't remember a time I enjoyed more than she and I merely relaxing in her feather bed, sipping some fine New Orleans coffee she'd brewed.

Finally, just before noon, seemingly with some reluctance, she dressed and went over to the saloon and returned with a plate of food.

"Where's yours?" I asked, admiring the eggs, pork chops, and hotcakes.

"I didn't think it would be wise to let anyone over there think I had company. Besides, you're my business, and no one else's, at least for a little while longer."

And I don't think I ever enjoyed a meal more, than partaking one while Lizzy Perlmutter watched me with eyes the color of a cornflower over a porcelain cup.

When I finished, she asked, "What am I going to do with you, Tag?"

"Doubt if I'll be around to be done with, Miss Lizzy, and am a little surprised I still am."

"You've seen the posters out on you?"

"I have."

"Tag, why don't you head west and we tie up in San Francisco, which I plan as my next stop, and where there's fifty thousand to hide out among... until this all cools down. You'd look just fine in a beard for a while. Like I said, you could sit shotgun—"

"Still got work to do, Lizzy. You wouldn't want a man around who didn't do what he said he was going to do."

"If you promised a spirit I guess you could break it, and I knew your sister if only slightly, and she seemed one who'd want her brother to live, and live happy...and it seems to me you've already done plenty to fulfill your pledge."

"Maybe, but I promised myself as well, and I promised Angel Sanchez...and the son's a' bitches killed the best damn horse ever to wear iron shoes and a dog that was a hell of a philosopher and smarter by a long shot than his master."

She laughed, and I smiled.

"Well, I guess I wouldn't care for a man who wouldn't kill several fellows over the loss of a dog and a horse."

My smile faded. "And a sister and brother-in-law and two beautiful nieces."

"You do what you think you have to do, Tag McBain. I never knew a man worth his salt who didn't do just that, even if a woman hates the fact."

"I'm truly sorry, Lizzy, as there's nothing I'd like better than to head for the sunset with you. This is not something I like doing, it's something I have to do."

She sighed deeply, then offered, "I'm going in to see what's up in the place. If I learn anything about what's up in town, I'll come back out and let you know. Meanwhile, you should get a little sleep before things liven up this afternoon."

I had the hunch she knew I was there for Colonel Dillon himself, and maybe that I knew he met with Bridgid Fimple every Saturday afternoon at the Mystic Hotel, then she stopped at her doorway, turned, and confirmed it.

"You'll make sure Bridgid doesn't get hurt?"

"Damn sure, if it's in my power."

She paused before she continued, and her voice got that same low quality that warmed my backbone. "And if you live, you'll head out to San Francisco?"

"Lizzy, that's an offer only a fool could turn down."

She nodded and left, closing the door softly behind.

My backbone continued to stiffen, and occasionally shudder, as I knew there was a fight coming. I could always tell I was getting near a battle when my mouth dried out and I didn't have enough spit to swallow.

Lizzy had a beautiful Seth Thomas clock in her drawing room, and if I looked at it once, I looked at it a hundred times as the afternoon wore on. I left the house only once and that was to grain and loosely saddle the gray. I'd given Jackson the mule to Angel and his brother along with a twenty dollar gold piece, as it was the least I could do for the boys, and wished them well with instructions to head out for the sheep county in south Arizona, or into the San Joaquin Valley of California, where I'd heard there were huge herds, mostly tended by Mexicans.

I wanted to be upstairs in the Mystic when my target arrived, so I set out down the back alleys at three thirty. I was only seen by one woman, who was smacking a rug hung over her line. She paid me little heed.

There was an outside back stairway to the upper floor of the Mystic, and I took little time in mounting it and, happily, finding the rear upstairs door unlocked.

By the spacing of the doors, I could tell the front two rooms were the largest, and knowing what I did of Dillon, new that he would select only the best. Both of them, to my surprise, were unlocked. So I flipped a coin, and entered the one on the left. Both had bay windows that stuck out over the boardwalk below, and the street could be seen for its total length. I presumed Dillon, even though he was having an assignation he would want few to know of, would enter by the front door.

The doors to the rooms were in slight indentations, and I'd opened the one I entered open just a sliver, but because of the recession it occupied I could only see ten feet or so down the hallway. To my surprise, I heard footfalls coming down the hall. It was my plan to take it as it came; if my room was entered I'd confront them then and there, if not, I'd wait until they were *in flagrante delicto*, if my Latin didn't fail me, or in flaming offense, otherwise well occupied at the task at hand. There was something about finding holier than thou Dillon with his pants hanging on the butler's valet at the end of the bed that appealed to me.

With my eye to the crack, I saw Bridgid Fimple in her skinny bony best enter the room across the hall. It seemed I was in luck. I hurried back to the front windows, and was not to be kept waiting long, as Colonel Mace Dillon came striding down the board-walk right on time. The hell of it was he had his nephew in tow. And both of them were heeled, each with side arms and the boy carrying a lever action.

That was good news and bad, as I had the nephew on my list as well, but I'd planned to make Dillon squirm for a good long time before I put one in his knee, one in the other knee, one in his person-als, one in his gut, and finally one between his lying eyes just to get him to quit screaming.

Then I wondered, was he bringing his young nephew along to give him a lesson in the fine art of pleasure women? Or worse, for some other illicit purpose? Nothing would surprise me.

Maybe the nephew was some kind of a lookout, and would wait downstairs, making sure no trouble came up the stairway.

Off course you couldn't see the rear stairway from downstairs, so I presumed he would accompany the Colonel up and perch himself on a bench at the end of the hallway, near enough to my door that one stride would put me on him.

Or maybe we would accompany the Colonel into the room with skinny Bridgid, or into the room I occupied. It could be that both of them would occupy separate rooms if they were to stay over until Sunday service. That brought a smile to me, thinking of them fresh from a visit with Bridgid to a visit with Preacher McGregor to cleanse their souls until they could soil them again.

And I proved to be right, as it was a murmur of conversation and two sets of footfalls coming down the hall. I didn't risk keeping the door ajar, but heard the Colonel instruct, "Wait here. Don't be going down for coffee or a damn thing. You watch the door. I don't want to be disturbed. You know what to do if that damned Slade shows his face."

"Yes, sir. I'll stay alert."

"Good."

Then I heard the door across the hall open and close.

I gave it fifteen minutes, by the mantle clock over the small fireplace in the fancy room I occupied.

Having no interest in alerting Colonel Dillon with gunfire, I flipped my Army Colt around and took a good grip on the barrel, opened the door standing so as to be out of sight of the bench and nephew, took a quick step out and caught him rising from the bench, looking as surprised as if a scorpion had been in his underwear and chomped down on his personals. The blow took him dead center in the forehead and he crumpled. I caught him and eased him to the floor.

I'd deal with him after my primary prize was taken care of.

I reversed the Colt, eased the hammer back, and tried the door to give Dillon and Bridgid a bit of a surprised, and found Dillon to be a prudent man. It was locked.

A boot to the door near the hardware took care of that problem with one hard blow from the sole of my boot. The problem then was trying to quickly recover from the pain that shot from thigh up my backbone to the back of my neck, feeling as if I'd been the one whacked in the head with a heavy revolver.

But the anger coursing through my veins made

me recover quickly and in two strides I was inside, to find Dillon scrambling, in the condition God had delivered him to earth, to grab for his sidearm, hanging on a doorknob to what I suspected was an adjoining room, and Bridgid sitting up in bed, the covers raised over her upper body as if she had something not seen by half the male population of Nemesis.

My best laid plans of a slow death were for naught, as he got a hand on his revolver and I had no choice but to let fly with a shot that took him in his prodigious gut, and spun him back against the wall, knocking a nicely framed sampler flying. But he still had weapon in hand. I had to pause as Bridgid went flying by, screaming for her blessed mother.

Dillon, to his credit, got a shot off but it was way wide. I shot him in the shoulder of the arm holding the weapon, again slamming him against the wall, and he dropped the revolver, and couldn't make up his mind to reach with his remaining good arm to cover his still erect phallus, for the shoulder wound, or to try and stop the blood pumping from his gut.

"You dirty bastard," he managed, convincing me to slow down the process.

"You ordered your scum to burn my sister out, and she and her husband and her two beautiful daughters died over a trickle of water."

To my surprise, he looked guilty, and suddenly remorseful.

"I did no such thing.  I ordered Cavanaugh to scare them off the place.  To accept my offer to buy the place.  The man reached for a weapon, and it got worse from there."

"That's a damn lie.  Ignacio Sanchez saw it all. Cavanaugh shot him down in cold blood."  He didn't respond to that, knowing that Cavanaugh would lie to him if the truth was better.  So I continued.  "Well, sir, you were, as the lawyers and judge would say, the proximate cause.  And I'm the jury and executioner at the moment, the only one at hand."

"I'll pay you—"

Now, that made me angry, and I fell back on my old plan, and pulled one off, blowing apart a knee. He collapsed, and again my plan went awry as he fell within reach of his revolver, and reached for it, which encouraged my next shot.  Rather than between his lying eyes as I'd planned, it took him behind his ear and put a goodly portion of his face across the wall behind.

He was no longer the well-dressed, well-groomed dandy.

I took a deep breath and walked out to find the nephew, Seth Rheinhart, recovering and sitting up on his butt, his legs splayed out in front of him.  His eyes were still rolling like a couple of buggy wheels, and his rifle was more than an arm's length away and his sidearm still holstered.

"You were there when the Bar M was burned?" I accused.

He shook his head, trying to clear it, and I gave him a moment. To my surprise, he began to sob.

"I was…I tried to stop it. Cavanaugh was crazy wild. He offered to shoot me down if I got in the way."

"How old are you?" I asked.

"Seventeen, come my next birthday…in a month."

"Did you take part in killing my folks, my sister—"

"Your sister isn't dead," he said.

That took me mid-chest as if he'd shot me with his lever action.

I gasped, sucking wind for what seemed a long time, trying to get that together in my head, then asked, "What are you talking about, boy?"

"Cavanaugh took her. Up in the mountains to a line shack where he would ride up a couple of times a week, taking supplies and such. She was burned, trying to fetch her daughters. The Indian had dragged her outside and held her down, to keep her from running back into the fire. Her hands were burned, but healed."

"Where is she now?" I demanded.

"Cavanaugh sold her."

"Sold her? You don't sell people."

"I only know what Cavanaugh told me. He was in his cups and bragged about getting two bundles of furs from a bunch of Piutes or Shoshone for her. He used her until he was tired of her hating and cursing him, then he sold her."

"When was this?"

"A couple of months ago."

I couldn't help but wonder if the band I'd run across in the lava country might have had her prisoner. I might have been able to get her then and take her back to the Salmon country with me.

The nephew was still blubbering and I could make out him saying, "God forgive me, God forgive me," over and over.

I holstered my weapon, contemplating if I wanted to shoot down a sixteen-year-old whelp, to go along with the seven I'd already killed.

"Son," I said, my voice quiet so he quieted himself, "I can only hope you've learned something from all of this."

"I told Wentworth, soon as Cavanaugh told me he had her captive...but he said I should mind my own business just like he was going to do."

"You told him?"

"I did. He made me promise that I would not tell my uncle or Cavanaugh that he knew anything about it, and I did...promise I mean."

"But Wentworth knew?"

"Yes, sir."

Then I heard noises from down below. Apparently Bridgid had put the town on me, not that I fault her for it.

I kicked the rifle into the room I'd occupied, and instructed the kid, "Throw that sidearm into the room, and back up to that bench and stay there."

He two fingered the sidearm out and threw it gingerly deep into the room, then backed up to lean against the bench.

I spun on my heel and ran to the head of the inside stairway coming up from below. Wentworth led the pack, huffing up the stairs, carrying the double barrel from my old office, fully cocked.

He was looking down, making sure he hit each stair.

"Wentworth!" I shouted, and he looked up in surprise, stopping midway up the staircase.

He made the mistake of swinging the muzzle up, and I shot him mid-chest. He yelled "Martha," as he flung his arms up and went over backward. I could see it was the last of his wife's fried pullets he'd enjoy. Both barrels of the scattergun went off, blowing a considerable hole in the wall, and I could see nothing but the disappearing backs of his followers as Wentworth rolled ass end over teakettle down the stairs, and his cohorts scrambled for cover.

I hit the back stairway, and even with my thigh sending messages to my head bone to stop and rest before the leg gave out, I took the stairs three at a time.

In a galloping limp I made the loafing shed behind Lizzy's house, sucked up the latigo on the gray, and pounded out of there at a dust raising gallop, without a shot being fired behind.

It would be a long ride back to find Knows-No-Horse and his people, and hopefully my sister. But I could make that journey now, as my business in Nemesis was finished. I had her journal in my saddlebags and I expect she'd fancy its return.

I wondered as I pounded on, following the Transcontinental tracks west to find my back trail to the Salmon country, would my sister enjoy a move to San Francisco?

I knew I would, and to my great surprise, thought it was one I might be able to make.

And now I should find the time and the peace to finish Mr. Twain's book.

I'm glad I'm again McBain.

I rode out at a cantor, a killer, a horse thief, a wanted man…and totally at peace with myself and what I'd accomplished.

## A Look At: Shadows Of Nemesis (The Nemesis Series Book II)

### BY L.J. MARTIN

When word finally reaches him that his sister and her family have died a horrid death at the hands of a cattle baron and his craven cowhands, Taggart McBain comes down off the mountain with bear traps, a double barrel coach gun, two LeMats, and a Winchester. He's on the hunt. When the task is done and blood soaks the Nemesis, NV desert, he receives a shock—his sister is still alive.

Now, with posters on every trail in Idaho and Montana territories, and a killer's price on his head, he's on the prowl. What he finds is an equal shock, but not so much as to those who hunt him. When the hunter becomes the hunted, there's pure hell to pay.

*AVAILABLE JULY 2018*

## About the Author

L. J. Martin is the author of over three dozen works of both fiction and non-fiction from Bantam, Avon, Pinnacle and his own Wolfpack Publishing. He lives in, and loves, Montana with his wife, NYT best-selling romantic suspense author Kat Martin. He's been a horse wrangler, cook as both avocation and vocation, volunteer firefighter, real estate broker, general contractor, appraiser, disaster evaluator for FEMA, and traveled a good part of the world, some in his own ketch. A hunter, fisherman, photographer, cook, father and grandfather, he's been car and plane wrecked, visited a number of jusgados and a road camp, and survived cancer twice. He carries a bail-enforcement, bounty hunter, shield. He knows about what he writes about, and tries to write about what he knows.